It's Just Business

ZAINAB ALHALWACHI

Published by Shush Books
Shush Books is a division of Shaherazad Shelves
shaherazadshelves.com
Copyright © 2025 by Zainab Alhalwachi
All rights reserved.
Our books may be purchased in bulk for promotional,
educational, or business use. Please contact your local bookseller
or Shaherazad Shelves or by email at publishing@
shaherazadshelves.com

First edition, 2025
Cover design by Alex Asfour
Interior art by Muhammad Assadullah
ISBN 978-1-960323-31-6 (paperback)
ISBN 978-1-960323-30-9 (ebook)

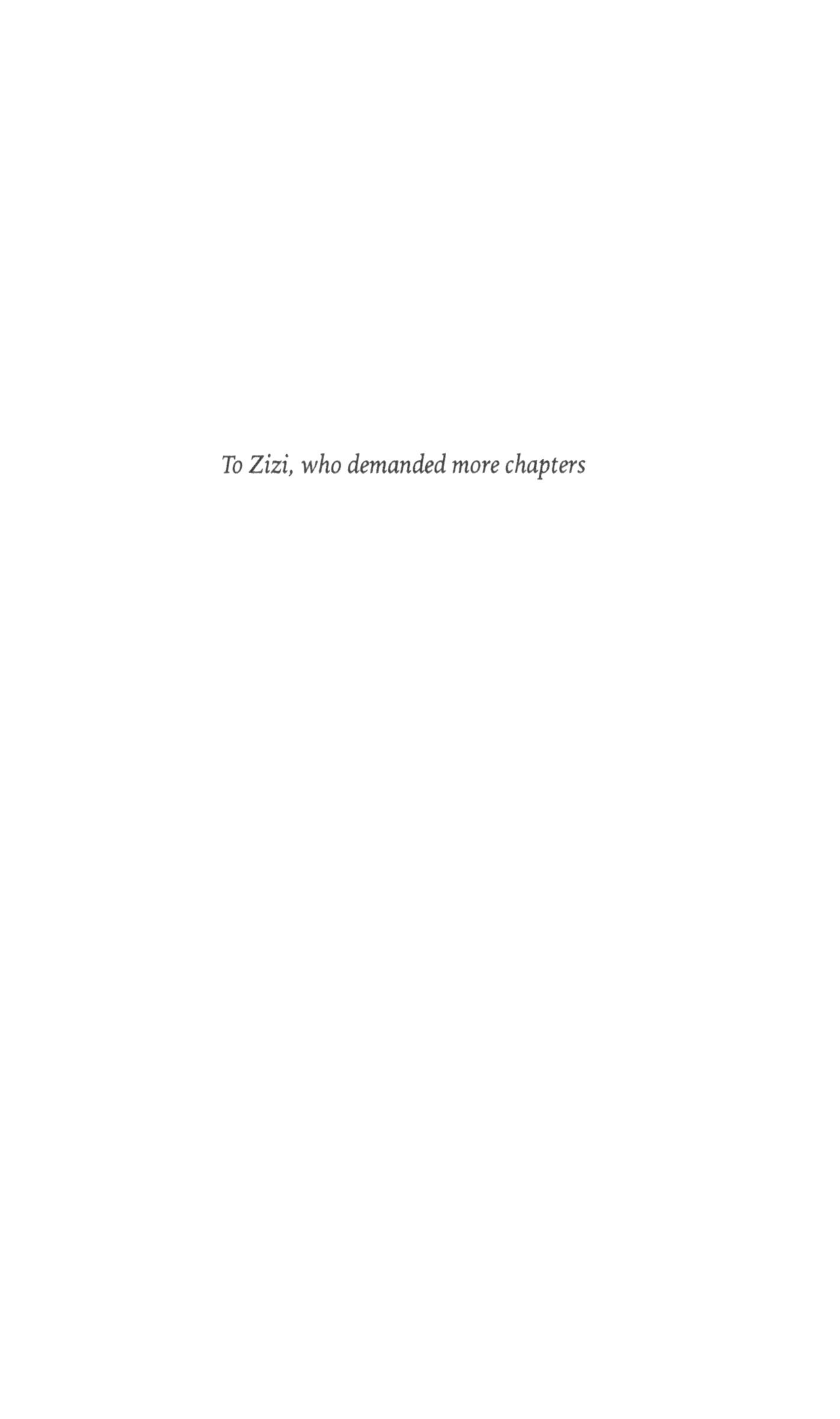

To Zizi, who demanded more chapters

CHAPTER

One

I've just landed in Dubai from a fourteen-hour direct flight from the 'States. After years of taking the same flight back and forth between my Ph.D. studies, those fourteen hours felt more like seven. People have told me I was crazy for taking the trip so often and dealing with the exhausting jet lag that accompanied it. But I couldn't help it. Dubai was a siren and I was the sailor lost at sea. I could not *not* visit every chance I got.

So there I was, in the back of a taxi making its way to the heart of Dubai between the high rises that flanked Sheikh Zayed Road. I loved this sight on this particular stretch of the highway. The tall buildings always felt to me like hopes and dreams were stretching out of the flat desert to touch the stars. And above me, higher than the buildings, I could see the five-day-old crescent moon. It didn't look so much like a moon as it did the sleepy eye of a dragon slit open just a little with the light of its golden eye pouring out. It looked like the start of a story, where jinn come out to play. It looked like molten gold. It looked like magic.

And I couldn't have been more excited to be back.

I especially had to be here for Ramadan. So, I took a leave of absence for a month, booked my ticket, and arrived on the fifth day of the holiest month of the year.

But Ramadan wasn't the only reason I was in the city. I had a meeting to attend—a big one. I've been putting off the job hunt post-graduation because I've set my hopes on this succeeding. If it did, I was going to have enough work to last me a lifetime, and it all depended on this meeting that no one—not my family, not my friends—knew about. I wanted to wait until everything was confirmed first.

So as the taxi made its way deeper into Dubai, away from the high rises and into the residential areas with houses hidden behind tall walls and yards decorated with palm trees, I looked at the moon and let myself get caught up in the familiarity of my surroundings. It was here that I was born and grew up, where I met and matured with my childhood friends, and where my aunts, uncles, and cousins meddled in my affairs.

Twenty-five minutes later, the taxi pulled up to my house. I had planned on calling my sister to open the door for me, but that wasn't an issue anymore. The garage door was already open and cars were parked all over the place. A quick glance at the models had me confirming that my family, *my entire family*, was here.

I wasn't expecting the family reunion for at least another day, but my parents clearly had their own plans. Not that I wasn't glad to see everyone. I love big family gatherings, but I was hoping to have some time to have my meeting before all the questions about my studies and future career started.

I may have been tired from the flight just a few minutes ago, but now my feet picked up the pace as I hurried to join the madness I knew was currently taking place inside my house. The gate was open since my parents were expecting my arrival.

The driver pulled in and parked in the open garage shaded with a wood awning so the cars could stay cool. I looked up at the sand-colored villa decorated with arched windows at the back of a small courtyard, our garden on the other side of the house with bushes and palm trees lining the wall. I paid the driver as he helped me get my suitcases out of the trunk. I left the suitcases at the bottom of the threshold steps and practically jumped over them to get to the door, flung it open, and hollered, "I'm here!" as if my presence wasn't enough.

The smell of what can only be freshly brewed gahwa greeted me, light gleaming off the golden dallah in the middle of the coffee table with dates and sweets spread around it. The aroma brought back all the memories of past family gatherings and events that started and ended with a cup of Arabic coffee.

"Noor!"

The shout came from every single person in the living room. My aunt and uncle, seven cousins, and my parents and siblings. I kicked off my shoes, readjusted my headscarf, and went inside to greet everyone. There was a lot of hugging and kissing and fist-bumping—for the guy cousins—going around, and when those were done, everyone moved to the dining table where the food was waiting.

Lots of food. It looked like each aunt had brought a dish they knew I loved. There was Auntie Farah's machboos, the spiced chicken steaming with spices and over red rice; Auntie Sara's kubba in labneh, the meat-filled fried bulgur wheat dough swimming in speckled white yogurt sauce; Auntie Maryam's dolma, the grape leaves stuffed with so much rice and vegetables they could burst; and Auntie Manal's macaroni. It was a mix of different Arabic food, but when there were so many delicious dishes from different countries, why limit yourself to just one?

The athan had already been recited while I was on my way here, which meant everyone had already broken their fast with dates, or water, or a stolen bite of food before praying maghrib. While the elders of the family took a seat at the dining table, my cousins and I took our plates and found a seat on the couches in the living room.

Everyone was quiet for a minute, shoveling food into their mouths. I took advantage of the stillness to appreciate this: the utter calm that came with being in a room full of people you love who love you.

But the quiet didn't last long. My cousin Ahmed asked, "Noor, how is your Ph.D. study going? What are you doing again? Chemistry?"

"Not chemistry. Genetics and molecular biology."

"So you don't know how to make drugs?"

"I could if you gave me a detailed recipe with all the numbers included, but I failed Chem 102 my freshman year of undergrad."

"Oh." After that, he went back to his food as if there was really no need to understand what I *did* do.

It was the same every time I visited. But I didn't mind. It was nice to see that they at least tried to understand what it was I did—no matter how many times I had to explain.

The thing with science in my family was that no

one really understood what a scientist does on a day-to-day basis. Tell them you do lab work and they all assume you're in a hospital doing diagnostic work. They can't envision the huge lab filled with rows of benches stacked with pipette tips and test tubes, the cell culture rooms with their counting and centrifuge machines, or the fridges and freezers filled with different chemical and biological reagents. And that's only in the genetics and molecular biology lab. It was a lot easier to just say, "I do research," and let them imagine what that entailed.

As I lifted another spoon of macaroni towards my mouth, one of my cousins, Hana, asked me, "Are you going to be here for the rest of Ramadan?"

"Yup, I go back two days after Eid."

"So, you mean we're actually going to have time to see each other this time?"

"We always see each other. I video call you more than I do my own mother."

"You know what I mean, loser."

I did know. Technology made it so easy to stay in touch with my friends and family at home when I was away, but at the end of the call, it was just me and a silent apartment. When you're physically there, at least there's someone to exist in the silence with you. But I couldn't let them know that the quiet was too loud. "Aww, does that mean you missed me?" I asked instead.

Hana gave a quick "No" before she went back to eating.

I grinned at her and turned my attention back to my own food. I was glad to be back. The last time I was in Dubai was three months ago, which wasn't that long, but it had been just for a week. It would be nice to at least have time to get over my jet lag for once.

One by one, people finished eating, and the table was cleared away. I was starting to relax. The dinner went well, and no one seemed overly suspicious about my abrupt arrival. When everyone was back in the living room and had a cup of tea in their hands, the long socioeconomic discussions began. I moved away from my cousins to pour myself a cup of gahwa, and, as I expected, a chorus of "Pour me some" came hurtling at me. So, I picked up the dallah, filled cups with coffee, and handed them out.

About halfway through my second cup, my eldest uncle, Ahmed, addressed me, "Any big plans while you're here, Noor?"

Of course, the question I was trying to avoid would come from him. "No, 'amo. I'm just going to relax and enjoy my time off."

For my highly successful CEO uncle, who was always rushing between meetings and planning the next big thing, this was not a satisfactory answer.

But I couldn't tell him the truth. At least, not yet. I had to make sure that my meeting went well first. I could see Hana and my sister watching from the corner of my eye. I avoided their gazes. If anyone was going to figure me out, it was going to be one of them. Hana could always read my silences.

At the end of the evening, I stood by the door with my parents and said goodbye to our guests. We collapsed on the couch, my mom, dad, two sisters, and I. We were sitting so close that at least some parts of us were on top of or under some of the others. And we sat like that, listening to the silence that spoke of missed nights, old history, and I love you's. It was the kind of silence that washed over you and seeped into you and left you feeling whole. It was good to be home while I tried to make something of myself.

It started as a passing thought. Something that came about when I was first searching for a job during my junior year and realized I didn't have any real experience, and the utter frustration from the no-job-no-experience-no-job cycle drove me to imagine a place that would take on the inexperienced and nurture them into hard-working individuals. An institution that gave students the space to explore biology and pick up transferable skills that they could proudly display on their CVs. I wanted to be able to take these rising professionals in and give them a place that wanted to see them grow into top scientists in their fields.

There are many good universities with research in different fields of biology, but I found positions to be limited, and not everyone was willing to hire a research assistant. The research sector is continuously growing, and I wanted to be part of that growth with a dream of creating a place that was more than capable of handling a large influx of new students and graduates every year.

But at twenty-one, I had to face reality, and the reality was that no one was hiring an inexperienced biologist straight out of university. So, I changed my gears and applied to graduate school. I studied for the GRE, wrote and rewrote my personal statement so many times that I could still recite it four years later, and harassed my professors until they agreed to give me outstanding recommendation letters. Later that spring, I opened an email from Boston University stating that I was accepted into their human genetics and molecular biology Ph.D. program.

I spent the following days in a state of excitement and fear. I didn't know how to live on my own, away from the family and friends I had grown up with, but I also didn't know how to *not* be a biologist. And the only option I'd have if I stayed in Dubai was to get a job away from the field I loved so much. So, I sent in my acceptance and took off. I may not have stuck to my parents' 10 p.m. curfew while I was abroad, but I upheld the values they taught me. Not to mention that having my schooling in English for the past twenty-two years really helped me adjust to being in an English-speaking country.

It was at Boston University, almost 11,000 kilometers from home, where I gained respect from my peers, published a few articles, and realized that my long-ago passing thought might not be so unattainable.

So, I sent out an email with a very detailed proposal for a learning-based research facility. I explained how it would be state-of-the-art, inviting seasoned researchers from across the globe to carry out their studies in fully equipped laboratories. However, they would have to agree to take on inexperienced students as their assistants and train them. This would allow the research to carry on but also provide a platform for the students to gain valuable technical experience. When I was satisfied with my proposal, I sent it to prospective investors and business incubators. I never expected to hear back from them since I still didn't have experience running a lab, yet alone an entire facility.

But a month ago, I did. I received a message asking if I was available for a meeting. I, of course, said yes.

The morning after I arrived home, I was sitting in a waiting room, wearing the most professional outfit I owned and waiting to speak with the CEO of Dubai's most prestigious business incubator, HighRise, while my parents were at work and my sisters at university.

The incubator's main workspace was a large area with floor-to-ceiling windows that provided a stunning view of Dubai's towers. I was lost in a trance as I admired the morning sun reflecting off the buildings.

A moment later, a tall woman wearing the most gorgeous abaya walked into the room. The navy-blue robe was made out of light material and had a beautiful gold embroidery pattern that ran down one-half of the robe, from the right shoulder all the way down the sleeve and to the hem. It was left open with a matching plain cotton dress underneath.

"Ms. Noor Saeed?" she asked, looking at me.

I was the only person in the waiting room.

"Yes, that's me." I got up and went to shake the woman's hand. My palms were a little sweaty, but steady in my determination.

"It's nice to meet you. I'm Ghada Mohammed, the CEO. I'm glad you could make it. I must say I was quite excited about the proposal you sent us. Please follow me."

I was glad that Ghada turned away because I could not help the giddy look on my face. She was *excited* about the proposal? Honestly, when I sent it out, I didn't really think HighRise would get back to me, let alone be *excited*. There was a spring in my step as I followed her.

Ghada walked into a spacious room that was adorned with a beautiful cream Persian rug that took up the whole floor. The border design framed the central field, which had intricate floral and geometric motifs interwoven in delicate patterns. The windows were floor to ceiling and the thick cream fabric of the curtain was pulled aside to let in the morning sun. A sleek glass desk was set opposite the windows.

"Please, have a seat," Ghada said with a smile while taking her own seat at the head of the desk. "I was impressed with your proposal. It shows how much thought you've put into this project, which is surprising since most of the ones we receive are usually a page long with vague descriptions."

I was a little speechless but managed to croak out, "Thank you."

Ghada acknowledged it with a cordial smile, but in the next second, the smile fell, and she turned serious. Still friendly, but definitely serious. *That's her boss face.* I was terrified and impressed. I definitely couldn't flip my expression that easily. I'd have to practice.

"We've decided to approve your project, which means that you'll have all our resources made available to you. However."

Ah, here it is. *Take a deep breath, Noor.*

"Because this is a rather large feat you're trying to accomplish, you will need to pitch the idea to a venture capitalist to ensure you have the right sum to make this happen. We just can't do this on our own."

I nodded. That didn't sound too bad to me. I was sure that, given time, I could convince a VC to agree with my manifesto. But Ghada's tone was still making little alarm bells go off in my head.

"Ghada, if you don't mind me asking, there seems to be more to this?"

"There is. Sometimes, these VCs will try to change the strategy to ensure a return on investments. For this project to go forward, you'll both have to come to a happy middle.

And while we're willing to have all our resources available to you, we're not comfortable expending before we have a guarantee of funds from the VC." She paused and took a deep breath. I took one, too. "You'll have to get him to agree three days before Eid."

Eid was in twenty-three days. I had three weeks. So much for a relaxing Ramadan.

"Is that alright with you, Noor?"

She was giving me a choice: either I convinced some big-shot VC who already seemed to have a problem with my project to support it or take my proposal elsewhere. I took a deep breath to steady my nerves, calm my heart, and ease the stress that was building on my shoulders.

She didn't need to ask. There was never really a choice. I was going to make this happen.

"Yes."

The meeting with the VC was scheduled for tomorrow afternoon. Until then, Ghada had nothing for me to do. I was grateful. It was nearing four in the morning in Massachusetts, and I was bone tired this early in the day. So, I decided to head back home.

When I reached, I found everyone home but asleep, taking their midday naps after work. During Ramadan, working days finished early, giving everyone time to rest during their fasts before they woke up and started preparations for iftar.

I climbed the stairs to my room and collapsed on the bed, where I stayed, only waking for afternoon prayers and going back to bed until I was awoken by the athan for maghrib. There was a pile of papers and my laptop open to remind me I had a thesis to write and a proposal that needed to be foolproof, but I ignored them. I prayed and went downstairs to finally eat and see my family.

"There you are, Noor," my mother said as I got to the bottom of the stairs. "Were you asleep all day?"

"No, I woke up early and went out for a bit."

"Who with?"

I really should have expected the follow-up questions. I never learn.

"Just myself. There was something I wanted to check out at the mall." At least I wasn't lying while still fasting. I felt bad, but at least not as bad.

My younger sister looked utterly betrayed when she turned to me and asked, "Why didn't you wake me up?"

"Or wake me up?" my other sister added.

"Hessa, Sara, do you actually believe you would have woken up?"

"That's not the point!" they chorused.

Lord save me. I loved my two younger sisters to death, but they could be very unreasonable sometimes. Most of the time. OK, always.

"Girls, leave your sister alone. If anyone should have been woken up, it's me."

"Baba, you were helping and then you stopped helping." That got snickers from everyone at the table.

"Are you feeling your jet lag yet, Noor?" my mom asked.

"Just a little."

"Great, because your 'Ama Farah invited everyone over to her place tonight."

I was tired, stressed, and had some thesis editing to do, but I was away for long enough that I missed my boisterous aunts, goofy uncles, and ridiculous cousins. I wanted to see them as much as I could. I finished my food and went to get dressed.

I t was one-thirty in the afternoon, and I was already yawning. I was at the workspace that Ghada chose for my meeting with the VC. It was an open space in the heart of Dubai International Financial Centre fitted with desks and chairs and computer monitors with lots of windows that made the place airy. The windows should have also made the place hot, given how blinding the sun was outside, but the air conditioning was blasting through the space. I was just about to sit down when I received a notification on my phone from my best friend.

Heba: Is he there yet??

Noor: Nope, but I am twenty minutes early.

Heba: Don't be nervous! If you can convince Boston University to let you in without a master's degree, you can convince this VC to give you all his money.

Noor: Who said I was nervous?

Heba: You're there twenty minutes early. Of course you're nervous.

If there was one person I couldn't hide from, it was Heba. We'd been friends for over fifteen years. And even though she was kilometers away working on her own Ph.D., she knew every detail of my life. She was the one I harassed to proofread my proposal.

Noor: No one likes a know-it-all.

Heba: So you admit I know it all?

I was just about to write back a response to deflate her ego when someone rapped their knuckles on the table, making me jump and drop my phone. I bent down to pick it up but ended up smacking my head on the table. *Ouch.* I slowly sat back up and applied pressure to my forehead.

"Owwww." I could have sworn the table was further away.

"Are you alright?"

"Yes, I'm okay," I squeezed out despite the throbbing pain. I bent down again to pick it up, this time making sure I avoided the edge of the table. When I finally got my phone with no further injuries, I saw that I had another message from Heba and that the man was still at my table.

I looked up and asked, "Can I help you?"

"Hi, I'm Khalid. Ghada set up this meeting?"

Oh, Lord, help me. I didn't expect him to be so young. He looked like he was in his late twenties.

"Hi!" I got to my feet so quickly that I started to blackout and sway. I quickly caught myself on the edge of the table to keep my balance. When I got my vision back, I said, "It's nice to meet you. I'm Noor."

"Would you like to sit down, Noor? I don't usually have my meetings standing up." He smiled to show me he was joking, and I gratefully took the small peace offering. We sat down.

Since it was Ramadan, there were no drinks to order, hide behind, or fill in the awkward silence, so it was straight to business. Since I had already made a fool of myself, I needed to take control of the situation. It didn't help that my nerves had finally made an appearance. I took a deep breath to recenter myself.

"I first wanted to say thank you for considering my project for your next investment. I promise you won't regret it."

His eyes seemed to sharpen at that. "That's actually what I wanted to talk to you about. In almost every aspect, your project is something we wouldn't hesitate to invest in. It's smart, has growth potential, and fills a gap in the research sector." He paused and moved his hand as if he was going to pick up a drink, but probably remembering that he was fasting, he pulled his hand back from the empty spot and continued, "but the one very crucial factor missing from it is revenue."

Khalid looked at me expectantly, waiting for a response, except I didn't have one. That was the one thing I couldn't figure out. I wrote every detail I could think of in the proposal, finding ways to get scientists and students what they needed, but I couldn't find a way to make money out of it. I'm a scientist; my education in business is limited.

When I wrote my proposal, I left out the financial part, thinking I'd get back around to it, but then Ghada reached out, and a meeting was set within the week, and the next thing I knew, I was finalizing a project in the lab and hopping on a plane. There just wasn't any time.

He glanced at his watch, then his phone, then back to his watch. I could tell he was done with this meeting and ready to leave. But I couldn't end it like this.

I had nothing but my honesty.

"To be frank with you, Khalid, I don't have a plan for that yet."

He leaned back and crossed his arms. "Is that so?"

"Yes. But if you'll give me a couple of days, I will have something ready for you. I just need a little more time." I hoped he could hear the sincerity in my voice. Maybe the hint of desperation would help, too.

I couldn't tell if he was considering or getting ready to politely decline.

"Okay, Noor," Khalid said, leaning forward and pinning me with his stare. I noticed his hazel eyes as he went on, "I'm interested enough in this project to give you a few more days. I can tell how passionate you are about this, but the truth is, no one is going to invest without some sort of guarantee. It will cost millions to get this off the ground. I admire the fact that you want to give students real-life experiences. I'm interested. From a business perspective, it would be great to have our names on if it succeeds. But if it doesn't..."

"You need an exit strategy."

"Exactly."

I could understand that. It was business, not personal. I just had to buy myself some time to figure out how to get revenue. I could do it. I *had* to do it.

He must have seen my determination because my silence seemed to placate him. "Alright, Noor. Is there anything you would like to know about myself or the firm? What are you looking for in a business partner?"

This I had an answer to.

"The project needs a partner who understands the crux of its establishment. The institute is meant to be primarily educational. It isn't a money-making scheme, and a partner who is in it just for the money is the wrong partner."

We started talking about the institution and what we both hoped to see it become. I always imagined a large four-story building with more windows than walls. The space inside would be filled with natural light, the main reception warm and bright. Past the security turnstiles, you'd walk into an airy sitting area with different nooks and tables for people to gather and talk or work outside of their offices. The elevator banks would take you up to the main laboratory and office floors, which would be divided by specializations for different fields of research but accessible to all researchers when needed to promote collaborations. There'd also be separate rooms for student researchers, where they could feel like they belonged.

Khalid agreed four-stories was a good start. He even mentioned numerous universities he thought would be interested in collaborating.

"Wow, it's been an hour already," Khalid said as he glanced at his watch.

I could tell it was that long from the dryness of my mouth. I needed some water. But that would have to wait until sunset.

"There's another meeting I need to get to. Just so I have an idea of the time frame, when do you think you'd be ready to share your plan?"

"Give me three days."

"Great, I look forward to hearing from you then." I stayed seated as he collected his belongings and stood. "It was nice meeting you, Noor."

"You too, Khalid."

He gave me a small smile and left.

I had high hopes after the meeting. I could see his passion for the project as we spoke. It was kind of like he was a little in love with it, too.

CHAPTER
Four

I sat at the table, going over the implications of the lie I'd just told when I remembered Heba. I turned my phone over and was relieved to see that the screen hadn't shattered from when I dropped it. I had notifications from my sisters now, too.

Heba: Where did you go?

Heba: Is the VC there?

Heba: He is, isn't he?

Heba: Is he cute?

Heba: Will you be forming other partnerships as well?

Heba: Update me! Are we getting our institute?

Sara: Good morning, sunshine! Where are you?

Sara: Buy me a present. Ok bye.

Hessa: Where are you?

Hessa: Mona is asking if we want to go to her place tonight.

Hessa: I told her to count us in.

I responded to my sisters, telling Sara I would not be getting her a gift and confirming with Hessa about my cousin's. I conveniently left out where I was. Then I messaged Heba.

Noor: Ask me how the meeting went.

Heba: How did the meeting go?

Noor: Remember how we said the only issue with the whole idea was money?

Heba: Please tell me he didn't take back the offer because of that.

Noor: He didn't. I bought myself some time to work on the revenue plan.

Heba: You need Allah.

Noor: And a plan.

Heba: Do your best.

Noor: Thanks, I'll need to.

———

Later that night, after having iftar at my cousin's place, I dropped my sisters home and drove around Dubai for a little while. It was a freedom I missed when I was away.

I didn't have a car in Massachusetts. Instead, I often opted to walk or take public transportation.

But in Dubai, driving was the easiest way to get around town. And it was the best thing in the world. Dubai has three main highways parallel to each other that lead across the city. At the northern and southern borders of Dubai, these highways merge into one main highway that stretches to the neighboring Emirates. The highways are large expanses of concrete and are illuminated by street lights that keep the lonely traveler company late at night.

And tonight, that lonely traveler was me.

I made my way north on Sheikh Zayed Road, needing to see lights and skyscrapers. Hopes and dreams. Maybe seeing how other people did it would give me some inspiration for my predicament.

A half-hour later, I was still roaming the streets, and still without a plan. At this point, decided the only way out was to stall for more time. Three days might not be enough time to figure this out. But I had to, otherwise, I would lose his investment, and that was the end of my dreams, just a well-written proposal.

But how? He would ask for my revenue solution eventually. I couldn't just not tell him. Although. I got the craziest idea, but it might be stupid enough to work. I needed to run the idea by someone, so I called for reinforcement.

The great thing about Ramadan was that there

was virtually no curfew. Three in the morning became the new 10 p.m. Parents were more lenient, and husbands were out with their friends, so when I pulled into Lamya's driveway, I wasn't surprised to see that Maha and Aysha were already there. I walked to the side entrance door, and as I got closer, I could hear Maha asking for tea and Aysha yelling over her for leftover dinner.

I've known Lamya, Maha, and Aysha since middle school. We sat next to each other on the first day of seventh grade and haven't been able to get rid of each other since. The last to join the group was Heba.

If ever there was anyone who could help me carry out my plan, it was this group. I should have gone to them first. Now, as I walked through the door, I flung myself into the arms of the smartest, silliest, and most down-to-earth woman I knew.

"Quick, Maha, get the rope. If we tie her up, she can't leave us again," Aysha said as she held me in a vice-like grip.

Maha extracted herself from the group hug and went back to her tea, her hand resting on her stomach the entire time. At twenty-five, she was the most settled out of all of us. She had a stable job as a financial risk analyst, a doting husband, and her first baby on the way.

"I am not going to do anything until this baby comes out," Maha said.

"You're eight months along. Any sooner, and you'll end up having it in my living room," Lamya told her as she went to refill Maha's cup of empty tea.

Back when we were sixteen, Maha made us all make ten-year plans. We had to include all the things we hoped for ourselves. The only person who followed it to a T was Maha.

"It's not an *it*. It's a him."

"You said *it,* too," I teased.

"Someone, anyone, please feed me," Aysha said but was only really looking at Lamya to serve her.

"You know where the kitchen is," Lamya shooed her. Aysha didn't need to be told twice. She rushed out of the room.

"Wait!" I tried to stop her, but it was too late. "Guys, I need help," I said.

"With covering that bruise on your head? I thought you'd never ask," Lamya said.

"How did you hit your head anyway?" Maha asked.

"That's part of why I need help. Just let Aysha get back..." I trailed off, stunned to see Aysha return to the room already with a plate full of food.

"I'm back. Spill the tea."

So, I did. I told them everything, starting with the proposal's approval and the eventual meeting with Ghada and Khalid.

They listened intently as I explained my situation. "He said he would give me three days, but that isn't enough time, not when I've been racking my brain for months trying to find a fix for this problem and still have nothing to show for it. So my goal right now is to prolong the meeting with Khalid until I can figure this out."

When I was done, Aysha asked between one bite and the next, "Why didn't you ask me for help? You could have let me put my MBA to good use."

I knew Aysha had an MBA for the fun of it, but her career was in photography. And it was a good career, given the numerous galleries that featured her Dubai-inspired shots, showcasing the poetic juxtapositions between the shifting dunes and the rising metropolitan buildings.

"I was scared. I didn't want everyone to know, only for it to be rejected." I looked at them beseechingly, hoping they would understand why I kept this secret.

All at once, they smiled at me.

"We're so proud of you, Noor," Maha said in a soft voice.

I may have choked up, and my eyes may have filled with tears. Of course, they understood. We were more than friends—these people who I watched transform from girls to women, from students to career success stories.

I missed them. Sitting across from them now, I could already feel my heavy heart when I left again and missed having them around. Living alone did that to you. It made you feel things that you shouldn't be feeling simply because your heart was anticipating the moment when you would. Like foreshadowing heartache.

I shook off the feeling because I was here now, and I still hadn't told them my ludicrous idea. "Thanks, guys. It means a lot. And Aysha, since you have a fancy MBA, got any ideas?"

"Nope, you're screwed."

"That's what I thought. But I do have an idea that will buy me some time, and I'm going to need your help to carry it through." I looked around and saw patient faces. So far, so good. "I'm going to set up multiple meetings with Khalid throughout the next three weeks. And at every meeting, I'm going to need an emergency to come up. Something that will make it important for me to leave and reschedule the meeting. That way it'll seem like I intend on telling him my idea, but a series of unfortunate events will prevent it."

I stopped to catch my breath and gauge their reactions. They all had their thinking faces on.

Eventually, Lamya sat up straighter, and I could see the engineer in her go through things in her head when she said, "I think we can pull this off."

"If there is a plan that doesn't involve too much walking and has a bathroom nearby, count me in," Maha said as she got up and went to the bathroom.

I would tell her that all that tea couldn't be helping her bladder, but we all learned early on that you don't take away a pregnant woman's cravings. I looked at Aysha to see what she had to say, but I caught her with a mouth full of food. She nodded enthusiastically to indicate her agreement.

"Okay," Lamya started us off, "We have three weeks. I'm thinking we do two meetings a week, which means we'll need at least six fantastically absurd ideas and two more as extra precautions."

"We can use me as a fake labor emergency," Maha offered.

"That is diabolical. I love it," Aysha said in approval. "I, for one, think there should be food involved."

"It's Ramadan, there's no food during business hours," I pointed out.

"Then have the meetings for or after iftar."

I scoffed. Aysha was not one to be deterred.

"That might work in our favor. It gives us more ground for ideas," Maha chipped in.

"How am I supposed to convince Khalid to have a meeting outside of business hours?" I asked incredulously. "That can't be appropriate."

"As you said, it's Ramadan. The rules change. I'm sure he'll appreciate not working on an empty stomach," Lamya reasoned.

I opened up the notes app on my phone. "Alright, let's hash out our plan."

Around two in the morning, all the tea was drunk, the food devoured, and the floor littered with cards and game chips. I felt a lot better now that there was a plan to buy me some time, but I couldn't ignore the fact that I still had no idea what to do about generating revenue.

I spent the next forty-eight hours working on revising the literature review for my dissertation during the day and house-hopping at night. On the third day, I woke up at seven in the morning—which meant my jet lag was finally getting better—and sent Khalid an email.

I informed him that I was going to proceed with his firm for the project and that I would like to set up a meeting for tonight.

He got back to me a few hours later, saying he was okay with the time and place. Perfect. Now, all I had to do was confirm with the girls that Unfortunate Event Number One was a go.

I spent the rest of the day drifting between a state of anxiety and perpetual fear. I was about to trick a future business partner during a month when I was supposed to be my most honest and genuine self.

The plan was simple. Go to a coffee shop at a mall. Make small talk. Have the girls show up. Oops, emergency, time to leave. Simple. In theory.

Yet when I parked my car in Mercato's outdoor parking lot that night, the reality of the situation smacked me in my made-up face. I looked at my phone and willed myself to call everyone and cancel. Cancel the evasion plan with my friends. Cancel the whole meeting with Khalid. Canceling completely with Ghada. All of a sudden, it was too much.

And it would have been easy for me to make those calls. But the terrifying road ahead of me could lead to the most amazing future, and who was I to deny myself that?

I turned off the car, bagged my phone, and stepped out before I could give it a second thought. I made my way into the mall and the air-conditioning hit me as soon as the double sliding doors opened, cooling the thin layer of sweat that coated me during the short walk from my car to the door. If my nerves didn't kill me, the humidity would.

Tucked in behind the stores was a cafe where Khalid was supposed to meet me.

I approached the end of the line and pulled out my phone to make sure everyone was where they were supposed to be. Lamya, Maha, and Aysha would crash our meeting and extract me before any of the serious discussions could begin.

Noor: Where are you guys?

Maha: We're almost there.

Aysha: Lamya kept changing her abaya.

Lamya: They were all dirty. What was I supposed to do?

Maha: Wash them.

Aysha: Or wear pants like me.

Noor: Guys, that really isn't important right now. Khalid is going to be here any minute.

Maha: We'll be there in fifteen minutes.

Noor: HURRY!

"Hi, Noor," came a voice from over my shoulder.

I jolted at the unexpected sound and slipped my phone into my pocket before turning.

"Hi, Khalid." I gestured at the counter, "Coffee?"

"Yes, please." He rubbed his temples.

"You still haven't adjusted from the caffeine withdrawal?" Almost everyone who relied on coffee to function throughout the day suffered from caffeine withdrawal the first few days of Ramadan. I try to wean myself off coffee the weeks approaching the month to help limit the affects.

Khalid huffed a laugh. "No, not yet."

We reached the counter and the barista gave us

a friendly smile and asked, "What can I get for you guys?"

"I'll have a double shot espresso," I rattled off. I then made the executive decision to quickly pay for my own drink before we ended up in the let-me-pay struggle. The female/male dynamic was one thing but add on top of that that we were Arab. We'd be fighting over who gets to pay until the mall closed.

Khalid followed my lead and didn't say anything before he placed his own order. A flat white. We moved down to the pickup counter to wait for our drinks.

"So what is it that you do, Noor?" Khalid asked as the waiter placed our drinks on the counter in front of us.

"I'm pursuing my Ph.D. in human genetics and molecular biology from Boston University," I told him nonchalantly before I took a sip from my coffee.

Khalid raised both eyebrows. "Wow, that's impressive."

I smiled shyly. "Thank you."

We chose to sit at a large table near the entrance of the cafe, then sat with my back to the rest of the mall.

Khalid followed me, but I ignored him while I quickly checked my phone. Lamya sent a message saying that they were parking. Perfect. I just had to stall.

"So Khalid," I said as I interlaced my fingers and braced my chin on them with my elbows on the table, "do you absolutely love working for a VC firm?"

"Umm, yeah, I do." I watched him lose himself in the thing he loved and it resonated with me. "I find it really exciting to be at the forefront of new businesses. To know that I had a hand in helping small ventures develop into something truly remarkable. To watch as it opens new doors for the future." Then Khalid seemed to come back down to Earth. Back to this moment. He smiled sweetly and said, "Sorry about that," then looked down at the table and took a sip of his coffee.

I couldn't help myself—I stared. I watched as he swallowed and looked up, and our eyes locked, and on some level, I knew that we understood each other. On a business level. Purely business.

I can't say how long we would have stayed like that because then I heard Aysha scream out my name all the way from the entrance of the mall. I rolled my eyes, gave Khalid a mischievous look, and told him, "You're in for a treat."

I turned around and waved at my friends, indicating that they should join us. It wasn't exactly professional, inviting my friends to a meeting, but at this point, nothing was being kept professional. There was just too much at stake to take good old professionalism into consideration.

As we had agreed, the girls approached the table and immediately started pulling out seats and speaking greetings over each other, just like elder Arab aunties and grandmas would.

"Noor! I can't believe you're here, it's been so long," Maha said.

"How have you been? You have to come over for iftar one day. I won't take no for an answer," Aysha threw in.

"You have to come to mine, too! I have this amazing spiced meat recipe that you would love," Lamya contributed.

"How is your mom? Your sisters? It's been ages since I've seen them."

"How long are you in town for?"

"Did you hear what happened to…"

"There's this new restaurant in Jumeirah…"

"You won't believe what my brother's wife's sister's friend…"

And on and on they went, their words blending until you couldn't really be sure who said what. I contributed every now and then, but mostly I just watched and enjoyed the show.

Throughout the conversation, Khalid's face was a study in transition. First, he appeared awkward, then, finally, his smile made an appearance once he reached amused.

The word *unprofessional* crossed my mind again, but I was desperate. And this was fun. Maybe

Khalid was enjoying the never-ending stream of verbal vomit coming from my friends.

To my surprise, Khalid leaned a bit forward and caught their attention.

The girls turned to him. *Oh no.* This was not part of the plan. They were not supposed to ask Khalid questions. I tried to catch their eyes, but I may as well have not existed.

Aysha had an evil look on her face I knew very well as she plainly asked, "Who are you?" She, of course, knew exactly who he was, but he didn't know that. So at least she wasn't blowing my cover.

Khalid, for his part, looked completely unfazed as he gave her a charming smile and simply stated, "I'm Khalid."

"Just Khalid? Like, just Beyonce?" Aysha continued, her face deadpan.

We all snickered, including Khalid, before he said, "Khalid Saleh."

As entertaining as this was, I still needed them to get me out of there, so I started kicking at legs under the table. But either they were just straight up ignoring me, or I was kicking the table leg because none of them even flinched.

Maha stepped in and asked, "Are you single, Khalid?"

Oh my God, shoot me now. What are they doing?!

I directed all my focus on kicking them harder

under the table and only half-heard Khalid confirming that he was, indeed, single.

I finally got Lamya's attention. I made a bunch of facial expressions that I hope translated to *what are you guys doing so help me I will pour date syrup in your favorite shoes get me out of here before he starts asking questions.*

Some of it must have translated well because Maha straightened up and gasped, "Is that the time? My parents are expecting me at my grandmother's. Noor, love, since you're here, could you please drive Maha and Aysha back home? Thanks so much."

And with that, everyone stood. I stayed seated a little longer and gave Khalid my best I'm-so-sorry-this-is-happening look. But before he could say anything, I stood, too, and told him, "I'm so sorry about this, but I can't leave them stranded in the mall. I'll call you to reschedule."

Aysha interrupted him with a quick, "Bye, Just Khalid, it was nice meeting you," as Maha grabbed my arm and started pulling me along towards the door, not giving Khalid the slightest chance to object as we exited the building.

CHAPTER
Six

Once in the parking lot, we gathered behind Lamya's car so that no one—i.e., Khalid—would see us as he walked out of the front door.

We spent fifteen minutes doubled over, laughing and gasping for air. The plan was a long shot and probably the worst idea we had ever hatched, but it was *fun*.

The heat eventually won over, so we climbed into Lamya's car and switched on the air-conditioning.

"I can't believe that actually worked," I told them from my seat in the back.

"Noor, you did not mention that he was good-looking. I feel like that should have been mentioned," Aysha said.

"You're the last one to talk! I can't believe you

asked him if he was single. That was definitely not part of what we discussed."

"Well, we would have discussed it had you mentioned it!"

"How was that information supposed to help us with anything?" I retorted.

Maha chimed in, "The fact that you didn't mention it actually says a lot. Anything you'd like to share with the class, Noor?" Lamya leaned out of her chair some more towards the back seat and looked at me expectantly. They were all looking at me.

"Okay! He's good-looking, so what? Can we please focus?" I implored them.

But, of course, that did nothing to deter them. Lamya spoke first. "He actually started commenting on what we were saying," she said in wonder.

"That's bold," Maha added.

"He's funny. I like him," Aysha declared, giving me a look.

"Can we please get back to business?" I begged.

Maha finally took pity on me, "I'm actually shocked that he didn't try to get rid of us. Imagine how much of a disaster this would have been if he had tried to restart the meeting."

"I'm so relieved it *did* work. I am nowhere near close to developing an idea yet," I said.

Lamya looked at me worriedly. "How are you going to figure that out?"

I looked at the floor of the car as if I would find all my answers among Lamya's scattered shoes. She needs to clean her car. "I don't know," I said to them at last.

"Well, how does this kind of place usually get funded?" Maha asked.

"By national funds, universities, or private investors," I responded quickly. I had done enough research to know that much by now.

"Have you tried those other options?" This came from Aysha.

"I sent my proposal to a lot of those, but only one university got back to me saying they didn't have enough funds to take up something like this," I told her.

We all fell silent for a while, lost in our own thoughts. Finally, I spoke up, more determined than I had been earlier.

"I *will* figure this out. It's not a question of *if*, but *when*. I won't just sit back and watch this opportunity slip through my fingers."

They all gazed at me with silent approval. I knew they would never think less of me if I failed, but I didn't want to fail. And I wouldn't. So, I appreciated it when Lamya looked at me and said, "We believe in you."

Before I left the car and we went our separate ways, there was one more order of business to complete: I had to email Khalid before he emailed me in order to dictate the time and place of our next meeting.

I told him I would be busy due to the outburst he had seen earlier but would be able to have the meeting in two days' time. He emailed me back almost immediately, confirming that, yet again, he was willing to meet up after working hours. Whether he had no life or really wanted to seal the deal, I wasn't going to question it.

I said goodbye to the girls and got out of the car, making plans to see each other again soon. I stood by as Lamya pulled out of the parking space. Just as her car cleared the exit, I saw Khalid come out through the mall's main entrance doors. In full view. Which meant he could see me, too.

He was looking down at his phone, so I turned around to hide behind the next available car. Except there wasn't any—this side of the parking lot was empty. And my car was all the way on the other side. I should have had Lamya drop me off.

Panicking, I rushed to the exterior of the mall and pressed myself against the wall. This way, Khalid would only see me if he turned his head back in my direction. I held my breath and waited.

I must have done something to please God today because Khalid kept looking at his phone as he made his way to his car, which was parked directly to the right of the door. I was too far on the left for him to notice me.

I would have berated him for not looking where he was going, but then he would know I was there. I waited until he was in his car and pulled away in the opposite direction. He turned around the corner and was out of sight.

I let out a sigh of relief. I could have probably explained myself out of why I was still in the parking lot, but better safe than sorry.

I reached my car and turned on the engine, then just sat there. Our first meeting was successfully highjacked, but that only meant that the count-down had begun. I now had under three weeks to figure out a plan. Driving around wasn't helping and thinking about it on my own wasn't helping either. I needed fresh eyes.

I drove down Jumeirah and made my way to my uncle's house. I tried doing this on my own, and it's gotten me nowhere. It was time I started asking for real help.

Fifteen minutes later, I pulled up outside his house and parked the car. It wasn't that late, so he should still be awake. I let myself in and found all the lights on in the house. My uncle and cousins were definitely still up.

I made my way to the living room, where I heard noises coming from. I found my uncle's wife and his kids watching an Arab drama.

"Hi, everyone," I said as I exchanged cheek kisses with my aunt and two girl cousins, Asma and Fatima, and squished their younger brother in a big hug.

"Hi, Noor. How's your holiday going?" Asma asked.

"It's great. Especially seeing all of you again," I said, smiling as I accepted the cup of tea she handed me. I took a sip and it was like a balm to my weary soul. I leaned back against the couch to watch the rest of tonight's episode with them. It was only towards the end of the episode that 'Amo Ahmed walked in.

"Is the show done?" he asked.

"Do you not like this one?" I asked him. He looked at me like I had offended his mother.

"No. I like the one they put after this. This one has too much drama."

"The channel is called MBC Drama," Fatima reminded him.

"That doesn't mean they have to be so dramatic," he huffed and sat, sinking into the chair to get comfortable for the next show.

"Noor, is being here as amazing as living in America?" Asma asked me during the commercial break.

I was going to tell them the realities of living alone but caught myself and said, "They both have their own appeals." It was true enough. It was great being able to experience different ways of living and learning about different cultures and people, but if you were like me, you missed being home.

My uncle was silent a moment, contemplating what I had said. He turned to me and made eye contact, silently telling me that he understood everything I hadn't said. He asked me, "Is there something on your mind, Noor?"

His wife and my cousins all turned to me. The thing with being around people who've known you since the day you were born was that the slightest dimming in energy was noticed. And your business became everyone's business.

"I actually wanted to talk to you about something," I told my uncle. He was business savvy. If anyone could help, it would be him.

He muted the show. "I'm listening."

"Can we speak in private?" I looked apologetically at the rest of the family, hoping they'd understand. My uncle and I moved to his office before I opened the topic. "I've been working on this idea. I want to start a learning-based research institute. It's a recent idea, and I have someone who wants to back me up on it." I took a steadying breath and continued. "But my one issue is that I can't figure out how to generate revenue from it. I need all this money to purchase lab equipment, pay professors, hire support staff, build the facility, keep up maintenance, and so many other things. I have a way now to put money *into* it, but for that to happen, I have to have a way to get money out of it. The group investing will withdraw if I don't come up with something quick."

I looked at him helplessly. "I'm open to suggestions."

He crossed his arms and looked pensively down at the table. I knew not to rush him. Finally, he said, "Usually, for a business to develop income, it offers services. If it develops a product, it sells it. If it's a service, it rents it out. If it's a journal, for example, it takes subscriptions. I won't tell you I understand exactly how a research institute oper-ates, but if you follow those guidelines, I'm sure you'll come up with something."

Could it actually be that simple? It wasn't a definitive answer, not yet. But it was something. And I could work with something.

"I'm sorry I can't be more help. Science is just an area out of my expertise."

I wrapped my arms around him. "You were perfect." I stayed with him and my cousins for a while, watching Ramadan shows until my mom called to ask where I was. I said my goodbyes and left feeling lighter than when I arrived.

I woke up the next morning feeling energized. I had a new angle to look at my project, and I was ready to brainstorm ideas.

I packed my laptop and notebook and hopped into my car to find a study space. Most of the cafes I liked to work at were situated on Jumeirah Road —a long stretch of restaurants, shopping centers, clinics, and coffee shops. I drove straight there. Some cafes and restaurants remained opened during Ramadan to cater to those not fasting, such as tourists, non-Muslim residents, and Muslims who couldn't fast for medical reasons. By the time I got out of the car and entered the building, I was hot, the moisture in the air already condensed onto every surface of me. I could use a cold beverage, but since I was fasting, I ordered a muffin to eat after iftar.

The cafe was dim, the sun not stretching far enough through the space, which kept the area cool. I gazed longingly as I passed by tables with cold coffees and juices. The place was two floors high with faux leather black and brown couches and dining chairs strewn about. The reason why I liked this particular cafe was because of the distance between each table. the tables were spaced close enough that each floor could fit plenty of tables —so there was always a place to sit even when it was full—but far enough that I felt like I had my own little nook.

I sat on a couch near a socket and plugged in my laptop. I had every intention of brainstorming for the institute, but like with all big projects, procrastination took me in another direction.

I worked a full four hours to complete a large chunk of my dissertation. The discussion section was giving me aches and pains. It was easy to run an experiment but so difficult to sit with the results and explain to others why they don't add up with current research in the field. It wasn't the achievement I'd hoped for today, but it was a close second.

———

It was already noon. I leaned back on the couch and relaxed into the soft cushion. My eyes ached from all the journal articles I'd read. I closed them to rest for a while.

It seemed so straightforward for commercial companies to find a way to make revenue. All they had to do was sell their products. The only thing coming out of my research institute would be research. Information and articles that would be submitted to journals, hospitals, and universities. So how do I sell information? I needed to brainstorm with someone who understood how a lab worked and would be able to think of lab-related services, so I messaged Heba, the only other person I know after high school who has continued to get a PhD in genetics.

Free to brainstorm?

Always. What's up?

What if I started a journal and included paid subscription?

It's a good start.

But it'll take time to generate an audience that would want to subscribe to it.

You need something quicker.

Siiiiiigh

Back to the drawing board.

What if you're limiting yourself?

What do you mean?

I mean you've been looking at this
as an opportunity to start a research
facility. What if it was more?

What if you added another element?
One that could make money?

Oh, I need to go. I have a meeting
with my supervisor. Let me know
what you come up with.

I could always count on Heba to say something essential and then disappear. I sat in the cafe for another hour trying to come up with a new component for the research facility. The journal was still plausible, but it was small. I could try to develop a product, but I didn't have the slightest idea what I could make or how to make it. I only had until tomorrow for my next meeting with Khalid.

Whatever I decided on, I would have to tell Ghada or Khalid and see if they were still willing to back me with the new addition. Deciding I had done enough for the day, I went home.

The following night, I broke my fast and then got ready for the meeting. As I was getting dressed, my sisters came into my room.

"Where are you going?" Sara asked as she opened up my dresser drawers.

"Out," I answered vaguely.

Hessa went straight to my cupboard and

browsed through my blouses. "Is out near City Walk?" Hessa asked.

I narrowed my eyes at my sisters. The meeting I had scheduled with Khalid was at City Walk. But there's no way they could have known that. So, I answered cautiously, "It is, why?"

"Everyone's going out tonight, so someone needs to drop Sara off at auntie Farah's house," Hessa said as she held up a blouse against herself in front of my mirror.

"Which is near City Walk," Sara added unhelpfully, pocketing a tube of lip gloss. We all knew where my aunt lived obviously.

"Right, so since your plan is there anyways, you get to take her," Hessa finished, then she and Sara walked out without a backward glance, taking my things with them.

"Yes, I would be glad to drop Sara off!" I yelled at their retreating backs. "Thanks so much for asking!"

"You're welcome!" they yelled back in unison. I loved having sisters, but sometimes being the oldest was a test of patience.

An hour later, I pulled up at my aunt's house. Sara opened the door with a quick "Thanks," before she hurried inside.

I pulled away from the house and went to the main intersection. Directly across from it was City Walk. As I drove through the green light straight into the outdoor sprawl of restaurants, stores, and apartments, I marveled at the lights. In the winter, City Walk was a great place to come and eat outdoors, but since it was a humid late spring night, everyone was seated indoors with the air-conditioning on full blast.

I turned right and entered the underground parking. I quickly found a space and parked my car, then made my way to the elevator which took me right to the center of City Walk. People were rushing past me in every direction, trying to get out of the humidity. It was ten pm, so the crowds were just starting to fill up the restaurants and cafes.

I had messaged Khalid before I left the house and told him I would meet him at a certain point and we could walk to the cafe/bakery together. The meeting-highjack plan with the girls was that Khalid and I would be suddenly intercepted by Lamya and Maha before we reached the cafe. They would walk with us for some distance, and then Aysha would call Lamya, pretending to be her mother, and say there was an emergency and she had to go home straight away.

It was more or less the same plan as two days ago, but this time I would conveniently tell Khalid that I didn't drive to City Walk. So, Maha would insist that her husband would pick her up, and since I couldn't leave a pregnant woman all alone, I would graciously accompany her to the car, leaving Khalid behind.

There were a lot of flaws, but one could only pray that it would work out as planned. I turned around the corner into the main rotunda and saw Khalid propped against one of the building's support beams, looking at the crowd. He noticed me as I approached.

"Hi, Khalid."

"Hey, ready? Let's get some sugar and talk business." He started towards the cafe.

I followed, thinking to myself how much I was looking forward to *not* doing that. We were walking down one of the paths that had an alley from where Maha and Lamya would walk out of.

"So, Noor. You seem to have a fun group of friends," Khalid remarked. There was a warmth in his voice that told me he really meant it.

My smile came naturally. "Yeah, I like them," I replied. "What about you? What are your friends like?"

He chuckled at himself, and I could tell he held the same love for his friends as I did for mine. "My friends will be the reason I end up in prison, but they'll be the ones to also bail me out."

"They must mean a lot for you to keep them around then."

"They're like my brothers. I wouldn't trade them for anything."

I was just about to mention that I felt the same way about my circle of friends when I saw my sister and cousins come out of the alley that Maha and Lamya were meant to come out of.

At first, I didn't think anything of it. I was going to say hello to Sara and Aunt Maryam's four kids— my cousins, Ahmed, Mohammed, Mona, and Hana —until it dawned on me that I didn't know how I would explain Khalid.

I could convince my sister and female cousins not to say anything, but my male cousins would hold it over me forever. Either I told them that I was having a business meeting that could amount to nothing, or they would assume we were dating. I could tell them we were just friends, but there wasn't even a small part of me that thought they would believe that.

They hadn't seen me yet, so without thinking, I grabbed Khalid's arm and pulled him into the alley on our right. I wasn't really supposed to be touching him, but this was an emergency.

I caught him off guard, and he stumbled into me. I held him up and then raised a finger to my lips, signaling that I needed him to be quiet.

He gave me a questioning look but complied. I edged near the mouth of the alley and peered back at where my sister and cousins were.

"What's happening?" Khalid asked.

I turned around briefly to say, "I'll explain in a second."

I looked out again to watch for my sister and came face-to-face with my cousin's chest. Ahmed's younger brother, Mohammed, his sisters, Mona and Hana, and my sister were all standing slightly behind him, looking at me with amused expressions.

I looked up at Ahmed. He looked at me, then looked behind me at Khalid and asked, "What's happening?"

My brain stopped working. It was coming up with a hundred different options and didn't know which one to choose, so it chose nothing. I must have stayed quiet for longer than I thought because the next thing I heard was Khalid approaching my cousin and shaking his hand.

"I'm Khalid. It's nice to meet you," Khalid said. "Do you know Noor?"

"We do know Noor. We're her cousins, and this is her sister," Ahmed told Khalid in an intimidating voice. "We don't know you."

All I had to do to stop this train wreck was open my mouth and state that we were business partners. But then I thought of the revenue idea I didn't have and the possibility that this might still fail. I couldn't have them believe I had a business when it was still only a *possibility* of a business.

"I've only just recently met Noor myself..."

Khalid paused and looked at me, clearly confused that I hadn't said anything. He didn't know that I was keeping the business plan a secret from my family.

It was time I put my big girl pants on. "Ahmed, everyone, this is Khalid. He's my new friend."

If I thought Khalid was confused before, he definitely looked confused now. He gave me a questioning look, but I gave him a hard one back. I'd explain everything after my family left.

"New friend, huh?" Ahmed said. "Well, new friend, let's go play some laser tag."

Wait, what?

Ahmed threw his arm around Khalid's shoulder and dragged him back towards the indoor gaming center.

Notifications from the group chat popped up on my phone as I followed behind my cousins and sister.

Aysha: Where are you??

We've been waiting forever. I was promised food after this. I'm hungryyyy.

Did you not see my sister and cousins pass by you? They found Khalid and me and now we're being dragged to Hub Zero.

Aysha: What?!

Maha: We were a little late. They probably left the alley just as we entered from the other end.

Do you think that's enough of a
distraction or do you need us to
come?

I think it might be suspicious if you
guys showed up. I'll just roll with
this and see what happens.

Go feed Aysha.

Aysha: Unless in case of an
emergency, please don't call until
after I've finished eating.

Maha: She means do your best.
Update us.

I put my phone away and trailed behind Khalid. I was simultaneously trying to overhear what the guys were saying to Khalid and dodging questions from the girls.

"So, who's Khalid," Sara asked, grabbing my arm.

"He's a friend," I repeated.

Mona, Ahmed's and Hana's youngest sister, who was twenty-four years old, grabbed my arm on my other side. "Yes, you've said that already. But we've never heard of Khalid before."

"He's a new friend," I clarified. I thought I heard Khalid say my name up ahead, but I was straining to hear when Hana jumped into the conversation. Hana was twenty-seven and older than me by a year.

"The fact that you're giving us vague answers isn't helping your case. Is he your boyfriend? You know you can tell us."

I whipped my head around to her and stumbled on a step. I would have fallen flat on my face had Mona and Sara not been holding me. "He is not my boyfriend," I told them all exasperatedly.

"Do you want him to be your boyfriend?" Sara asked loudly—very loudly.

I saw Khalid cock his head as if he were trying to hear our conversation as much as I was trying to hear theirs.

"No, we both happened to be craving sugar, so we came to City Walk. It's no big deal." The lie flew easily out of my mouth.

"Yeah, okay, but why have you never mentioned him before?" Mona interjected.

"Because I knew everyone would get like this."

These three were obviously not listening to me. I could see them giving each other calculated looks.

"Is he single, though?" Hana asked.

Ahead of us, the boys broke out in laughter. Then they started shoving each other, grinning from ear to ear the whole time. They had apparently become best friends. I crinkled my nose at the sweetness of it. Why bromances were so endearing, I had no idea. Also, it was possibly a very bad idea to let it happen.

"Nooooooor, helloooo, are you there?" Sara was poking me hard between my ribs.

"What? Yes, what?" I swatted her hand away. "Stop poking me."

"Is he single?" Mona repeated for Sara. They really weren't going to let this go.

"Yes, okay, yes. Please leave me alone and don't bring this up again, I beg you."

We reached Hub Zero after what seemed like an eternity later but was probably only five minutes. We caught up with the boys at the counter as they were buying tickets. I inserted myself between Khalid and Ahmed.

"Hey, I'm so sorry about this." I looked at him apologetically. "There's no way I can make them go away anytime soon."

He smiled and said, "It's okay. I haven't played a game of laser tag in a while." He looked over my shoulder at Ahmed and Mohammed. "And your cousins are nice."

"I'll have you know, I'm actually really good at laser tag."

"Is that a challenge?" he asked with a menacing gleam in his eyes.

I forced myself to look away. This side of Khalid was fun, and I think I could lose sight of what this partnership was if I wasn't careful.

"You're on." I turned to Ahmed, "Put me and Khalid on separate teams."

"Way ahead of you," Ahmed said. "It's going to be me, Khalid, Hana, and Sara against you, Mohammed, and Mona."

"Why are we only three players?" Mona asked.

"Because we have the best two players on our team," I said, looking first at Mona and then giving Khalid a pointed look. He crossed his arms and smirked.

Game on.

We split the bill equally for one game and made our way to the laser tag room. My team entered the briefing room, and as Khalid and his team came in, he 'accidentally' bumped into me, making me stumble a few steps. "Oops, sorry, Noor," he said sarcastically. His uninhibited grin almost made me stumble again.

The game was so on.

The instructor came into the room and showed us how the game worked, explained the safety rules, and how to put the vests on. Once we were all ready, we entered the game room.

It was a maze with random wall barriers interrupting movement in all directions. You couldn't tell who would be hiding around the corner.

Mohammed, Mona, and I went to our base at the far end of the room while the others went to their base near the door. Having played with my cousins before, I knew Mohammed would try to be the leader, and Ahmed would definitely be the leader on the other team. I also knew that absolutely none of us were going to listen to them.

When the buzzer for the game went off, we charged ahead. Mohammed, Mona, and I took different routes. I navigated through the maze, catching flashes of people as they took corners and ran for enemies in their sight. I stayed near the edge, away from the mayhem. My strategy was to make my way to the enemy base and charge at them from behind.

Everyone was so absorbed that I got to the other end quickly with no hits on me. I snuck up to the base and shot Sara, who was looking in the other direction, and while her gun turned off for being caught, I ran through the center of the maze, catching both Khalid and Ahmed running back to their base. With a competitive grin, I saluted Khalid on my way back to home base.

Mohammed and Mona saw what I'd done and raced past me to chase Khalid and Ahmed back to their base, taking shot after shot while their guns were out.

I raced back to base and waited until Mohammed and Hana returned. They rested for a second, then rushed back into the maze. I followed the same tactic as before and edged toward enemy base. This time, there was no one there.

I ducked into the maze and found my three targets, all with their backs exposed to me. I shot their backs, then raced past them and turned around to get a few shots at their heads. They kept shooting at me, but their guns weren't working. That didn't deter them, though.

They chased after me. I took them past our empty base and through the maze. Their guns recharged, and they shot at me, effectively taking my gun out of commission. They kept after me as I ran to their base. I was now backed up against the wall.

Unfortunately for them, they didn't notice Mohammed and Hana sneaking up from behind them. Their guns shut off when they were shot in the back, and I took off. My hijab slipped just as Sara rounded the corner and shot me, and then she blocked me from view so I could fix it back in place.

The rest was a beautiful, chaotic mess.

People ran, and people chased, and Khalid painted a bullseye on my back, so I painted one on his in return. We were pounding feet and screams and curses with the beep of our guns as our constant companion.

At the end of the game, the same buzzer that started the game ended it. Boos and hollers went up. Mohammed, Hana, and I high-fived and made our way to the door. Sara and I reached it at the same and we both forced our way through, pushing the other to get out of the way. The same was happening with the other members doing the same thing to each other behind us.

It had been years since I was here long enough to play a game of laser tag or do anything adventurous with my cousins. I missed it, missed being with them and finding random things to do just to spend more time with each other. It reminded me of lonely nights in my apartment, watching my cousins on my phone screen hang out, even if it was just watching a movie at home. Now, watching them, I was glad to be here.

Once we were all in the briefing room, Khalid stood next to me. We looked up at the screen and saw my name on the top and Khalid's somewhere in the middle. I couldn't help myself; I looked at him with a clear I-kicked-your-butt grin.

He refused to look at me, still staring at the screen when he said, "Do not say anything."

"I beat you," I told him.

He sighed deeply and then made eye contact with Ahmed over my head. "I thought you said we could beat her," he demanded.

"I said if we took another player, we *might* be able to beat her." Ahmed sighed deeply, too. "That didn't work too well for us."

Khalid then looked down at me. "I admit defeat."

"Admit defeat? I made you eat defeat for breakfast, lunch, and dinner. I made you swallow defeat like medicine. I am the maker of the defeated."

Throughout my rant, Sara and our cousins gave me blank looks and left the room. Khalid stayed.

When I finished, he poked me sharply in my side.

"Ouch! What was that for?"

"Your ego seemed like it needed deflating," he said with a lopsided grin.

"Ha ha," I deadpanned.

"Come on Maker of the Defeated, let's go congratulate the rest of your team."

We exited the briefing room and found everyone arguing outside.

"What do you mean why was I targeting you? You were the enemy!" Hana exclaimed.

"But I'm your sister!" Mona retorted.

"My *enemy* sister!" Hana threw her hands up in exasperation.

Mohammed stepped in and said to Mona, "I shot you because you ate the last gaimat tonight."

"You're not helping," Sara informed him.

In my opinion, those delicious small, round fried doughs immersed in date syrup were defi-nitely something to seek revenge on.

"Wasn't trying to help." Mohammed grinned and crossed his arms as he took a step back.

Ahmed stepped in and tried to put a stop to it

but his voice only added to the others and made the scene much louder. People were staring.

To my surprise, Khalid moved from my side, approached Ahmed, grabbed him by both shoulders, turned him around, and walked away. I think the suddenness of the movement caught Mona and Hana off guard because they looked in the direction that the guys had just left and followed. Sara, Mohammed, and I weren't ones to argue with this new, quiet development, so we followed, too.

Mohammed ran ahead to catch up with Khalid and Ahmed. And even from where I was walking in the back with Sara, I could hear them talking and see them shaking from laughter.

"You're staring," Sara said.

"No, I'm not."

"Mmhmm."

I ignored that.

We made it to the doors of Hub Zero, where Khalid was simultaneously shaking hands and one-sided-hugging Ahmed and Mohammed. He turned to Hana, Mona, and Sara and gave them high-fives.

Finally, he came my way, and I moved us away from the rest of the group.

"Thank you for going along with everything," I told him.

"No worries. I had a good time, so thank you," he said, but then his brow furrowed. "But, Noor, as much as I liked you calling us friends, I have to ask

—why didn't you tell them that we're business partners?"

I glanced over my shoulder. "I'll explain everything. Just not when we can be overheard." Also, after I had time to analyze the I-liked-you-calling-us-friends part.

Khalid didn't miss a beat. "Okay," he said with more patience than a normal human being could possess.

"It's late now, so how about we raincheck on that meeting?" I asked.

"Can't wait." He gave me a sweet smile and walked away, waving at everyone's chorused "Bye, Khalid" before leaving through the doors.

I was walking alongside my cousins and sister when Lamya messaged.

> I heard what happened from Aysha
> and Maha. You haven't said
> anything yet. What happened?

> We played laser tag.

> You played laser tag?! He didn't ask
> about your revenue plan?

> I think he was too busy becoming
> best friends with my cousins.

Should I ask?

No, let's just leave it at that.

Ahmed was informing his
teammates of every single tiny
movement that cost them the game.
Mohammed and Hana were
complaining about how annoyed
they were to have to fast while
studying for finals.

Well, it wasn't the plan but looks like
it worked anyways.

Believe me, I am going to pray extra
hard in thanks tonight.

Come over tomorrow night?

Yes.

I'll let the others know.

Please have warag enab.

I already have the grape leaves
ready for stuffing.

I put my phone away and walked along quietly, listening to my cousins' banter and letting their voices float and wrap around me. Dubai was bustling with people, the night was warm, and city lights softened the world in its glow. I looked up and saw the moon and constellations I could not name. I took a deep breath and soaked in the City of Life. The plan was working, although not exactly according to plan. Regardless, I had Khalid right where I wanted him.

Nine

I heard very little from Khalid in the next few days. I had sent him an email asking when he would be free for our next meeting, but he never got back to me. I wasn't too concerned. I was sure he had other business to attend to, and I wasn't going to complain about not hearing back from him. Not when it helped give me more time.

I was already a third of the way done with Ramadan and was starting to feel time slip away from me. So, I spent those days moving from house to house, staying as late as was socially acceptable before returning home to eat with my family before fajr prayer.

I didn't work on my dissertation, I didn't send my supervisor any progress updates, and I definitely didn't work on a revenue plan. And even though my responsibilities were a constant hum in my mind, filling me with nervous energy, I still enjoyed the time with my family and friends.

Three nights after the laser tag game, I was playing carrom at my aunt's house with my cousins and sisters. By the third game, I was sorely losing, so I sat to the side, watching Sara, Hessa, Hana, and Mona play. Mona and Sara may not have been the best at laser tag, but their chip-flicking skills were so intense that their pieces usually ended up flying off the table. Hessa and Hana had more finesse, which meant that they usually won. They all certainly kicked me out of the game easily enough.

I was biting open another sunflower seed when Sara pushed her chip hard enough to bounce off the edge of the table and sent it flying toward my face. I was so used to this occurring that I easily dodged the chip and opened up the seed at the same time.

Sara got up to collect her piece just as Ahmed and Mohammed walked into the living room. They ignored us and sat in front of the TV, talking to each other. We were too busy with the game to be affronted by the lack of greeting. Hessa was taking a shot at one of her chips, and I took a sip of my tea when I heard Ahmed saying, "…and Khalid said he could get us in."

"But do we want to go to a tent just to play cards again? Let's do something else," Mohammed replied.

"No way. I need to redeem myself after losing to Khalid for the past three days in a row."

I gasped and ended up choking on my tea. So *that's* where Khalid had been the past few days. I knew he and Ahmed had gotten on, but I didn't think they'd be making plans already.

And then I realized that Ahmed and Mohammed were being friendly with the potential investor, who I was currently tricking into believing I had a grand plan for my little institute, who I had also not yet explained that I was keeping the whole project a secret. This was a disaster waiting to happen.

"But he's going to be here tomorrow night to play cards again anyways," Mohammed groaned.

I choked on my tea again. Apparently, drinking tea and eavesdropping at the same time was a hazard. The girls took note and gave me questioning looks. Hessa raised an eyebrow and asked, "Did you forget how to swallow?"

"Ooooh, this is because they're talking about Khalid?" Sara singsong whispered, having finally overheard what the guys were talking about.

"Who's Khalid?" Hessa asked excitedly. We were all speaking in low voices now.

"He's Noor's boyf—"

"Shhhhhhhh!" This was going to get way out of hand if I didn't explain everything to them. Especially since Khalid was now Ahmed and Mohammed's real friend. I drained my tea and told the girls to follow me to Hana's room. It was about time I stopped hiding the truth from them.

Once they'd all shuffled in, we settled on the bed. "So," I started off, "I decided to start a research facility. I submitted my proposal to a business incubator and heard back from them just over a month ago."

"What?!"

"Oh my God!"

"That's amazing!"

I picked at the bed covers to hide my smile. I couldn't lie, it was nice to finally share my plans. "Thanks, guys."

"So what's Khalid got to do with this?" Sara asked.

"Khalid is the investor that I need to persuade to basically invest in the business."

"Oh my God, we called him your boyfriend!" Mona exclaimed. We all cringed.

"At least he didn't hear," Sara mused.

I gave her a hard look. "Didn't hear? You practically shouted it."

"He couldn't have heard because he was too busy being buddy-buddy with Ahmed," Hana contributed.

"Wait, when did all this happen? I'm missing something." Hessa looked wounded.

We told her about what happened at City Walk. I explained that I was hiding from them in the alley,

Sara explained how Ahmed dragged us to Hub Zero, Mona explained the laser tag game, and Hana added useless commentary. When Hessa was all caught up, and everyone understood the deal with Khalid, I told them the rest of the story on the plans I'd made to stall for time. They laughed so hard at what the girls and I did in Mercato that I had to hit a couple of them on the back to get oxygen back into their lungs.

The laughing lasted a while because every time they calmed down, they would look at each other and burst out laughing again. I was so relieved to have them filled in on the situation. Them laughing took a lot of the stress out of the whole ordeal.

Hessa wiped a tear. "So, do you have a plan yet for revenue?"

The dreaded question. The only thought floating in and out and around my head like and annoying mosquito. I had been avoiding it these past few days, but now with Khalid brought stark back into my reality, it was time to get to business.

Which reminded me—that Khalid hanging out with my cousins was a very possible reason why he hadn't bothered to answer my email about when to have our next meeting. I received an email notification on my phone just then.

To: Noor Saeed
From: khalid.saleh@venture.ae
Subject: Proposal Meeting

Hello Noor,

I hope you've been well. I apologize for not answering your previous email sooner. I've been a little preoccupied.

I'd like to propose that we have our next meeting this Monday. Does that work for you?

I'm excited to finally hear about your idea - knowing you, I'm sure it will be brilliant.

Best wishes,
Khalid Saleh
Junior Venture Capitalist
Venture AE

Yeah, I'm sure he was busy being preoccupied with *my cousin*. But it was hard to complain when I read and reread the compliment he slipped into the email.

I caught myself grinning and tried to stop. *Keep it professional. The girls were here, too. I'd never hear the end of it if they caught me smiling at a message from Khalid.*

To: khalid.saleh@venture.ae
From: Noor Saeed
Subject: RE: Proposal Meeting

Hi Khalid,

Yes, I've heard from Ahmed about your ventures. As to our meeting, I am happy to do it on Monday. I look forward to seeing you then.

Best regards,
Noor Saeed

The girls were reading over my shoulder as I responded. Now that they knew my dilemma, I could feel my anxiety multiply by five. I realized from the other day that our schemes weren't going to work. They were mostly variations of the same scenario: Khalid and I go somewhere, and the girls show up. Khalid would catch on. He wasn't stupid.

So, this was it. In three days, I had to either come up with something or come clean to Khalid. The tension must have been palpable because everyone was quiet.

"What are you going to do?" Sara whispered.

"I don't know. I've tried to think of different business models. 'Amo Ahmed said to think of products or services, but what can a research lab offer? All it has is space." I paused. The facility would have a lot of space. "What if I offered up the space?"

"To who?" Hessa asked.

"To anyone who wants to rent a lab." The anxiousness I felt before was disappearing. "Maybe pharmaceutical or biotech companies who want to do research and development?"

I looked at my sisters and cousins as the idea sank in. There are moments in your life when you run around and around in circles, not knowing what you're looking for, but chase it anyway. Then, all of a sudden, when you least expect it, it finds you instead.

The entire time I was thinking of an actual physical product, I forgot that the entire facility could be the product! And it's true most of the pharmaceutical companies only had their business departments in Dubai. Inviting them to use the facility for their research and development departments at a lower cost could open up doorways that would help a lot of people.

"Sounds like it could make decent money that way," Mona agreed.

"It could. I just need to contact companies and see if there's any interest, but if there is, then I think this could work."

With a grin, I snatched my phone and announced, "I have to tell Khalid."

I opened my email app and found another email

from Khalid waiting.

To: Noor Saeed
From: khalid.saleh@venture.ae
Subject: RE: Proposal Meeting

I hope only good things.
Let's say 2pm?

Best wishes,
Khalid Saleh
Junior Venture Capitalist
Venture AE

Now that I had a solid plan, I didn't mind when or where the meeting would be. I quickly confirmed with Khalid, excited to finally lay the groundwork for our partnership and discuss the how and who and when. It was a relief.

As we got up to grab a midnight snack, a sudden giddiness took hold of me. I was excited for my project, but I was also excited to see Khalid.

CHAPTER

Ten

After Hessa's throwaway comment about *who* I could rent the facility to that quickly became my salvation, I returned home and spent the rest of the night on my computer, going through articles, and crunching numbers.

Thoughts of Khalid would keep coming back to me. I'd only met him a few times but his small gestures stuck: how he'd chatted with my friends like they were his own, his silly bromance with Ahmed, how much he believed in my idea. He would be a great business partner.

When Monday arrived, I was anxious all over again. Khalid and I had decided to meet just before the end of the work day, which, since it was Ramadan, was cut short to three in the afternoon. Our meeting was at two.

As I was getting ready, I thought of all the

things I wanted to say today. I drafted a document that explained the rent idea and the theoretical revenue that could be generated. According to what I'd found, it seemed like a solid plan. However, I wasn't a business whiz. There might have been something I didn't consider that would affect the validity of the whole thing.

I took a deep breath. Overthinking wasn't going to solve anything. I just had to believe that the research I'd spent all weekend cultivating would bear fruition.

I went downstairs and was met with an empty living room. Everyone was either at school or at work. I smiled to myself. The room was devoid of people, but it was filled with so much life. My sisters' house slippers were by the door where they had switched them for sandals. My dad's coffee cup was sitting on the table in front of the TV. My mom's abaya was on the couch, where she had probably exchanged it for a different abaya last minute. It was a room still in motion, only on pause, waiting for its people to come back. I thought of my apartment in Massachusetts.

I rented an off-campus, two-bedroom apartment meant to accommodate my family when they came to visit. When I first moved in, it was freeing. Empty. I had furniture, but the apartment felt more like a showroom than a home. A few months later, my family came to visit for a few days, and they brought with them a whirlwind of activity and noise. I finally *wanted* to go back home at night. When they left, they took everything with them. My apartment didn't feel like a home anymore.

I tried to fill the emptiness after that. I recreated the chaos that had existed. I overstuffed the couches with pillows, pulled my furniture closer together, and bought more cookery than a single person needed. I made friends, good friends, and I would invite them over. We would talk and eat and make a beautiful mess, but at the end of the night, I would clean up, and all that would remain were my things. Just me and my things. A stark reminder that I was alone.

Now, looking at all *their* things, I felt sorry for myself. For the loneliness I would feel when I went back. It doesn't get easier. Not even after four years.

I shook the thoughts out of my head. I would only have six more months before I was moving back for good. I grabbed my keys and left the house, a little of the sadness still lingering.

The meeting was taking place twenty minutes from where I lived, not far at all by Dubai standards. In fact, it was the same cafe where we had our first meeting. I parked in the visitor's parking, paid to have the spot for an hour, and walked between the buildings. It was hot, but I used the distance to re-center myself. I needed to pull myself together. I was about to give probably the most important pitch of my life. I took deep breaths, focused on the world around me, and went over my idea again. By the time I reached the cafe, I was sweating from both the heat and my nerves. I didn't want to disappoint my family. There was so much pressure now that my sisters, my cousins, and my friends were all rooting for me. Ever since I was young, I knew they expected me to succeed because they knew I was smart. They did it out of love, but that same encouragement sometimes made me feel like failing wasn't an option.

I pushed open the door and immediately caught sight of Khalid. He was seated at the same table as last time. His back was to me, and he was staring at his phone, but I was still too fresh off the self-pity boat. So, I simply approached the table and sat without fanfare.

"Hi, Khalid." I must have sounded more dejected than I thought because Khalid gave me a puzzled look as I settled across from him.

"Hi, Noor," he said slowly before brightening a little bit. I gave him a small smile. "Noor, what's wrong?" He sounded so concerned.

I sighed. A small part of me wanted someone to know I wasn't okay. "I'm not in the best head space right now." I shifted my focus to the table and paused to think about how much I wanted to reveal. "I only have two weeks until I have to catch a flight back to Massachusetts. I'm just sad that I'll have to go soon." When I was done, I looked up. Khalid looked lost in thought.

I backtracked quickly, trying to act nonchalant. "Listen, I'm sorry I unloaded like that. Just forget I said anything."

"It's okay. Really. I'm happy you felt comfortable enough to share with me. We haven't been friends for long." Here, he huffed out a laugh. "Can I ask you though, have you told anyone else this?"

"No, of course not."

"Why 'of course not'?"

"Because. They would just worry. I've been there for years and everyone thinks I'm okay, and really, for the most part, I am. I just sometimes get kind of lonely."

"So, you're single then?" The question seemed to jump out of his mouth without his permission.

He looked thoroughly sheepish while I felt my cheeks flame and hoped he wouldn't notice. A part of me was excited that he'd asked, but he probably didn't mean anything by it.

"Yes, I'm single."

"Sorry, that wasn't any of my business," he said, but I thought he looked pleased.

"It's alright. It's only fair since Aysha stuck her nose in your business." We chuckled.

"How is Aysha? And, Maha and Lamya, right?"

He remembered their names.

"Good memory. They're great. Still as chatty as

ever. Actually, if you don't mind, Maha said she'd stop by to say hello. Her office is just around the corner." I gave him my best please-don't-kill-me look.

"No, not at all." Khalid grinned. "She terrifies me a little bit. I kind of felt like she was going to put me in the naughty corner that day in Mercato."

Out of all of us, Maha was very mommy. So while she made us clean up our messes, she was also kind, and loving, and caring.

"Honestly, she probably would have if you said one wrong thing," I told Khalid.

He grew serious suddenly. "Noor, I'm sorry you've felt alone. That you still sometimes feel alone. And I'm sorry that I don't have the words to make you feel better." He didn't look awkward, just upset—for me. Maybe even upset that he couldn't make me feel better.

Khalid might not have been able to, but I could. I was responsible for my own happiness. I counted my blessings and shook off the negative feelings that had been daunting me since before I left the house.

I needed to lighten the mood, so I smiled and went for a topic I knew would work for sure. "How's Ahmed?" I asked. Ahmed was my cousin, but at this point, I think Khalid knew more than I did. Khalid grinned from ear to ear and I couldn't stop my own smile at that.

"Ahmed's a great guy. He's so easy to be around. We actually ended up having friends in common."

"So I take the relationship is blooming? When's the wedding?" I teased.

"It's six months from now. Ahmed wanted to have it sooner, but I told him it wasn't reasonable. We need more time to prepare everything."

"Very logical. Ahmed is not one for logic."

"Not at all. It took a while to convince him, but he came around eventually."

"I'm very happy the two of you found each other."

"We have you to thank."

"Actually, you have Ahmed to thank. I had no intentions of running into my cousins at City Walk." We shared a laugh.

"Speaking of, you never told me why we were hiding that night and why you didn't tell them we were working together."

Maha showed up before I could start explaining.

CHAPTER

Eleven

Maha approached us with all her pregnant glory. Normal people would be sitting at home, waiting comfortably on their beds, but Maha wasn't like that. She couldn't sit and do nothing for months on end. So, she decided to continue working up until a week before her due date, which was two weeks away now. Everyone fought with her about it, but once her mind was made up, there was no changing it. When I told her I was meeting with Khalid today to give my pitch, she insisted on being here.

Khalid must have noticed me looking over his shoulder. He turned around to see what I was looking at and caught site of Maha. He gave her an enthusiastic wave. She gave a small wave back. She couldn't fast in her condition, so she had a snack from the counter in her hands.

"Hi, Noor. Hi, Khalid," she greeted us as she took a seat to my right. "How is everyone doing on this beautiful day?"

Khalid quickly glanced in my direction, a question on his face. I shook my head slightly. He understood. I turned to address Maha.

"We're great, my love. How are you feeling? You're very cheerful," I remarked.

"I am. Please ask me why."

Khalid and I shared an amused look before we turned back to her. "Why?" I asked.

"Because in two weeks, I will no longer be pregnant." She gradually raised her voice until she was almost shouting the word 'pregnant.' It was the loudest I'd ever heard her be. Khalid looked as startled as I was.

As if she didn't say anything, she took a bite of her pastry. After she had swallowed, she asked, "So what were you guys talking about?"

"I was about to explain to Khalid why we ended up playing laser tag with my family." I told her.

"Don't mind me," Maha said. "Pretend I'm not here." She continued taking small bites of her pastry.

I turned to Khalid. "There's not a lot to tell, really. No one in my family knows that I submitted a proposal, let alone got a response from a business incubator. Well, Mona and Hana and my sisters now know. But they didn't when we were at City Walk. I wasn't ready for them to know, so…"

"You pretended we were just friends." Khalid completed the sentence for me.

"Exactly."

"Do you always keep your cards close to your chest?" he asked.

"Of course. You don't win the game by showing your opponents your cards."

Khalid looked thoughtful for a second. "I hope you don't keep your cards hidden from me. I'd like us to be open with each other. Especially when it comes to our business."

"As long as we're on the same team," I said, but the term 'our business' replayed in my head. That confirmed that he was the right person to build the research institute with. I was certain that he believed in it. He believed enough that he had already convinced himself it was happening and it was ours.

He smiled. I smiled back. Maha looked at each of us in turn but didn't say anything. Khalid got a notification on his phone.

"Sorry, just let me respond back to this," he said as he started typing. Maha caught my eye, and I gave her a questioning look. She shook her head and took another bite of her pastry.

Khalid was frowning at his phone and typing with force.

"If you hit the keys any harder, you'll smash a hole through the screen." He didn't hear me. I tried again. "If you keep frowning, you're going to look sixty-five when you're forty-five." He looked up at that. I raised an eyebrow at him. "Are you vain, Khalid? Worried no one will want you if your good looks fade?"

"I moisturize and apply sunscreen daily." He patted his jaw. "My good looks aren't going anywhere."

Maha snort-laughed. Khalid put his phone down and looked across the table.

"So, Noor," he grinned and rubbed his palms together, "ready to give me your pitch?"

"Yes," I agreed enthusiastically. After spending so much time worrying and stressing and trying to find a solution, I was excited to finally share it. If he agreed after this, my insane idea would finally become an insane reality. In a few years, people will drive by the building and wonder at its architecture and what grand things were going on inside, the same way I passed by buildings now and marveled at them.

But before any of that could happen, Maha stood abruptly. "I have to use the lady's room. Don't say a word. I want to see Khalid's reaction when he hears." She looked at Khalid. He nodded, and it amused me to know he took Maha seriously.

"You'll love it, it's genius," she added before she waddled away.

"Is that the draft?" Khalid pointed at the file that had been resting on the table the entire time. I looked at it and smiled fondly.

"No," I said.

He raised a brow. "Then what is it?"

"It's my baby."

He made to reach for it. I pulled it away.

"Noor! Show me."

I pulled it completely off the table.

"Since you asked so nicely, no."

"Don't you think I've waited long enough?"

"Please incur the wrath of Maha on your time. I, for one, fear for my life."

"When you put it that way..." He chuckled.

"I'm glad you see sense. She's on her way back anyways."

Maha had a hand on her stomach and the other on her lower back as she made her way to us. I got up and went to her. I put my arm around her back and lent her my support.

"Are you alright?" I asked her.

"No. Yes, well, I will be," she said calmly as I settled her on the chair.

"Maha, are you sure? You're pale." Khalid had a point.

As I looked at her face, I noticed she was very pale. That raised all kinds of flags as I studied her face.

"Maha, what's wrong?" I implored her, concern making its way into my voice. She was very still, but she looked calm as ever.

"I'm fine. Sit down. Tell Khalid your idea." Just as I was about to call BS, her hands suddenly gripped the edge of the table and her knuckles went white from how tight she was holding on. She focused on the table and took small, even breaths.

Khalid and I shared a concerned look. I sat facing her and took hold of one of her hands with both of mine.

"Maha, love, tell me what's wrong." My voice demanded an answer. Her other hand, which had still been gripping the table, finally eased, and she leaned a little back in her chair. Her breathing became more even.

She squeezed my hand. "My water broke in the bathroom."

My eyebrows pulled together. At first, I didn't get it. She didn't carry a bottle of water with her when she went to the restroom. But then realization struck me so hard that I was completely incapable of stopping myself from smacking my forehead with equal strength. The sound it made echoed in the spacious cafe.

"Maha!" I shouted. Both Maha and Khalid jumped. "You need to go to the hospital!"

Her calm was unnerving. I was pretty sure I was

panicking enough for the both of us while Khalid looked like he was a deer caught in the headlights. He sat frozen. We were quite the trio.

Maha squeezed my hand again and said, "Don't be silly. It's too soon to go to the hospital. You still have time to give Khalid your pitch."

She was calling *me* silly? She was going to deliver the baby in the cafe if she didn't start moving.

Maha squeezed my hand and the table for a third time as she went through what I finally comprehended was another contraction. She made a soft grunt, and the sound spurred Khalid into motion. He shot out of his chair, his own face pale enough that I thought he might actually faint.

"I'll go get my car," he said and ran out of the cafe.

Maha and I looked after him and then laughed at his sudden departure.

"Don't make me laugh," Maha said between giggles. "It hurts."

When the giggling subsided, I collected my things and her things and helped her get up. As we made our way outside, I instructed her to call her husband and mother. The pain must have been effecting her because she listened without any objections.

We slowly made our way to the curb, stopping every now and then when Maha flinched. All things considered, I thought she was handling her labor quite well. Although her grip on my hand never eased.

An SUV pulled around the corner and came to a sudden stop in front of us. The window rolled down, and I saw Khalid in the driver's seat. I opened the back door and helped Maha in. I climbed in behind her. Once we were in, Khalid asked which hospital and Maha told him Latifa. I wasn't surprised. That was the hospital where she was born, so it made sense that she decided to have her baby there as well.

Khalid sped away from the curb and took off. It was only ten minutes to the hospital, but Dubai International Financial Centre, where many companies were situated, was busy on a good day. With it being the end of the workday, there were more cars than usual on the road. It was slow going until we hit the highway.

Throughout the car ride, Maha clenched and unclenched her hands, squeezing mine in the process. I don't think I knew what I was saying to her, but I kept talking. I don't remember a time when so many useless utterances left my mouth. In addition to my senselessness, Khalid was adding his own remarks to the mix.

"It's okay, Maha, you're fine."

"You're going to be okay."

"Just squeeze my hands."

"Don't think about anything. Focus on your breathing."

"Do you need anything?"

"Look how great the day is."

"Just breathe."

Eventually, Maha snapped, "WILL THE TWO OF YOU PLEASE BE QUIET." Khalid and I immediately stopped talking.

"I'm sorry, I think we're nervous," I told Maha while patting her hand.

"You're nervous? I'm about to give birth. To a baby. Out of my..." she stopped, remembering Khalid was in the car. He pretended not to hear, focusing very hard on the road in front of him, but I could see from my position that his face was red. I would have teased him about it, but Maha squeezed my hand again, this time grunting in pain.

"I think they're getting worse," she said.

"That's good, right? It means it's coming?"

"If it comes any sooner, I will be having it in this car." I didn't think she was joking.

Khalid maneuvered the car into the exit lane for Latifa Hospital.

"Maha," he addressed her as he got us safely on the exit ramp, "as much as I admire you for going through this ordeal, please, don't have your baby in my car."

"Khalid," Maha replied, "I appreciate the lift to the hospital, but if you don't hurry up, I will not only have my baby in your car, but I will make you cut the umbilical cord, too."

Khalid looked like he was going to be sick. I snickered.

Maha's threat was unnecessary because five minutes later, we reached the hospital. I noted Maha's mom's car as we passed by the parking lot, which meant her husband was probably already there as well.

Khalid pulled up outside the doors of the emergency room, and I sprang into action, opening the car door and helping Maha out.

I shut the door behind us, and Maha leaned against the car while I went up to the passenger side window.

"Do you mind waiting?" I asked Khalid. "I need a ride back to my car." I could have technically ordered a car, but I was still excited about the pitch, and I spent the whole weekend wondering if it was good enough and I don't think I could have waited another day not knowing. If we drove back together, then I could give him at least a short version of it.

"Yeah, of course. I'll wait in the parking lot until you're ready. Just call me when you're done. Take your time."

"I don't actually have your number."

"Oh. Here, give me your number."

I rattled off the digits and watched as he typed

them into his phone and then pressed the call button. My phone rang.

"Now you do," he said with a smile.

"Great, thanks."

"Can we please go now?" This came from Maha who apparently had waited long enough and pushed herself off the car and started walking towards the door. I gave Khalid a quick glance and waved before I hurried to catch up with Maha. For someone in labor, she moved really fast. I put an arm around her back and helped her into the hospital with a skip in my step.

Auntie Nisreen was anxiously staring at the door when we walked into the hospital. As soon as Maha and I entered, we were smothered in hugs and kisses and the scent of strong Arabic oud. I've known Auntie Nisreen for as long as I've known Maha. There were times when I was at her house more than my own. Now, as I handed her Maha, she patted my hand and sent up a prayer that she would one day see me married and expecting. I usually joked about it, but I let her have her moment this time.

Near reception, I could see Maha's husband talking to the nurses. One of them had a wheel-chair. I walked with Maha and Auntie Nisreen and helped seat Maha. Before they whisked her away, they gave me a moment alone with her.

She grabbed my hand. "I'm scared, Noor."

What can you tell someone who is going through something that is incomprehensible to you?

I held her hand in both of mine. "I won't lie, Maha. I don't know a thing about giving birth or being a mother. But there are things that I do know. I know that it rains in the desert. I know that mountains have roots to anchor them. And I know that you are capable of more than your fear dictates. Especially you, Maha. So I want you to take a deep breath." We both took deep breaths. "And when fear tells you 'no,' I want you to tell it 'Yes.'"

Maha sniffled, and I wiped the tears from my eyes.

"Allah iysahil alaish wa itgomeen bisalama." I bowed to kiss her forehead before the nurses came over and took her away. Her mom and husband thanked me before disappearing around a corner.

I took another deep breath to get myself under control. As I made my way towards the exit, I sent Khalid a quick message letting him know I was done. He had been lucky and found a parking just opposite the door, so I walked over quickly.

I knocked on the passenger side window and heard the sound of the door unlocking. I opened the door and caught Khalid sliding his phone into his pocket.

"Hey. All good?" He asked as I put my seatbelt on.

"Yeah, all good. They took her to get settled in."

"Great, that's great."

"So, listen. Can I give you my pitch now? I would really like to know your thoughts."

He kept silent as he focused on merging with the main road. I opened up the navigation app on my phone and put in my car's location, then set it against the car stereo.

"So," Khalid started as he finally found space to merge, "your pitch. I'd love to hear it."

"Okay, great." I stretched towards the backseat, where I left the draft and grabbed it. Khalid glanced at it as I settled back.

"Are you sure we shouldn't call Maha so she can hear the pitch, too?" he joked.

"I think Maha will forgive us this time." I opened the file and quickly scanned what I'd written. "Okay, so. You already know all about the research facility and that my main objective is for it to be a learning institute?" I raised my voice towards the end, forming the sentence into a question.

"Yes. The main issue is revenue."

"Right. So, even though the research facility is a place for students to gain practical skills through internships, the facility will still be a fully equipped space with state-of-the-art technology that can be used for any type of research. While principal investigators will be working with students and other researchers to carry out experiments for their own scientific work, a portion of the lab space can be rented out to other companies.

"If you think about the numerous pharmaceutical and biotechnology companies in the region, you'll notice that a lot of them only have their business headquarters in Dubai. They don't carry out any laboratory work. One reason is that it costs too much to build a lab. If we built them a lab, they could rent the space and bring their scientific investigations into the region. I actually called a few companies over the weekend, and they were very interested in the idea."

We were almost to the car lot. Khalid was quiet in contemplation. I couldn't read his face and had to grudgingly admit to myself that his poker face was better than mine.

Eventually, he gave me a knowing look.

"What?" I demanded.

"Nothing," he said, "it's a great idea. But I know you didn't have this idea all along. When did you figure it out?"

"What are you talking about? Of course, I've known all along."

He raised an eyebrow. "No, you didn't. I knew from our first meeting. He pulled into the parking lot. "Which one's yours?"

Defeated, I pointed at my car. "It's this one." He parked beside it. "Well, if you knew I had nothing all this time, why didn't you say something?"

"Because I like this idea. And I admire you. And I admire what you're trying to do. I wanted this to work, so I gave you time to figure out a plan. I'm assuming you have some numbers for me to look at?"

My hands were shaking. I silently handed him the file.

"Great, I'll take a look at these and get back to you about what our next step should be." He smiled. "Good job, Noor."

A sudden laugh escaped my mouth. I turned in the chair slightly so that I was angled toward Khalid. "Thank you." It didn't convey the magnitude of my gratitude, but it had to do.

I grabbed my things and opened the door. Khalid waited until I was seated in my own car before he left.

And just like that, I was the CEO of a research institute. Minus all the fancy papers that made it legal and binding, that is.

I stared straight ahead, not really looking at anything. A breeze passed by, and I saw a piece of white paper stuck between my windshield wiper flutter. I got out of the car, and just as I figured, it was a parking ticket. I overstayed the one hour I paid for before the meeting.

I got back in the car and turned the engine on, clutching the little white paper the whole time. I looked at it and burst out laughing. I would usually be bothered by a parking fine because it could be so easily avoided. But, at that moment, I didn't care. It was well worth it. I think I'll frame it.

At a traffic light, I sent out messages to Maha, Lamya, Aysha, and Heba on our group chat.

Guess who's building a research institute?

Aysha: I knew it!

Lamya: AAAAAAH I'm so happy!

Heba: YES YES YES!

Aysha: Celebration at my house tomorrow night!

Heba: Not fair! I want to be there.

Lamya: Where's Maha?

She's in labor!

Aysha, Lamya, Heba: WHAT?!

Crazy story, Khalid and I had to take her to the hospital after her water broke.

Aysha: Ummm?

I'll fill you guys in on the details tomorrow.

Heba: Call me too!

You don't even have to tell us.

I switched groups and sent a similar message to Sara, Hessa, Mona, and Hana. Almost instantly, I got replies of excitement and congratulations back from them.

The drive home was fueled by euphoria. The towers looked a little taller, the cars seemed to be driving a little faster, and the sun shone a little brighter. To my delight, I saw my parents' cars parked in our garage when I finally reached home. Sara and Hessa wouldn't get out of classes until an hour later, but they already knew the news.

I rushed in and almost tripped on the steps in my hurry. I found my parents in the kitchen. My dad was wrapping sambosas as my mom fried the gaimat for iftar. They looked up and greeted me. I quickly kissed their cheeks before I settled at the kitchen table and told them the whole story. They were so absorbed in it, and I was so busy telling it that we all forgot about the frying *gaimat* until an excessive amount of smoke drifted by us.

When I finished recounting the events of the past two weeks—minus the scheming—they sang praises and kissed my cheeks and told me how proud they were. Five minutes later, I was receiving similar remarks from multiple aunts and uncles.

Oh, the bittersweetness of the Arab Hotline. Tell one person one thing, and two minutes later, the entire globe knows your business. In this case, I didn't mind so much since I was planning on telling everyone anyway.

Throughout the rest of the time until *iftar*, my parents asked me more detailed questions about the facility, the business incubator, and the investor. After we broke our fast and prayed maghrib, we all packed in one car and drove to my aunt's house.

The atmosphere was even more jovial than usual. From the moment I entered the door, I was fending off kisses from aunts and uncles and answering every question that came my way. This included questions like 'What do you do in a research facility,' 'Is it part of a hospital?' and 'Can I get free prescriptions.' At the end of the night, there was cake. The word 'Congratulations' was written in frosting. I'd been keeping everything a secret for so long that it was strange to have it celebrated.

As I was getting ready for bed later, I received a text from Khalid.

> Hi, Noor. I'm so sorry to be messaging you this late, but do you think it would be possible to meet tomorrow at noon? It's important.

He didn't mention what the meeting was for, so

I assumed it had to do with the next steps in the development process. Maybe even go over what we would tell Ghada. My deadline was in a week's time, but I didn't see why we couldn't tell her earlier and set things in motion.

I sent Khalid a quick message back, telling him that I was happy to meet with him. As I settled into bed, I felt a wave of contentment wash over me. Everything was finally falling into place.

Thirteen

I woke up to an email from my supervisor letting me know that the pages I'd sent her for my dissertation the other day were well-written, which put me in a great mood. That was fifteen fewer pages that I wouldn't have to edit later on.

I got ready for today's meeting with Khalid and hopped into my car. I turned the engine on and grinned when I saw that someone had already filled the tank for me. I retraced my route to DIFC since we were going to meet at the same cafe as the previous times. As I passed over the bridge on Sheikh Zayed Road, I thought of how the roads were completely remade. The highway was expanded by the work of dedicated and hard-working leaders and immigrants, the lanes raised into a bridge, and the canal redirected to flow underneath. How simple it seemed for this city to remake itself. How easily it could redirect its path. The thought had me pushing the car a little faster, now eager to reach the cafe and start talks of building and purchasing and hiring.

As I pulled into the parking lot, another car was coming out of a space near the entrance. I quickly signaled, worried that someone might come and park because I didn't claim it first. Gratefully, the driver didn't take long to exit the parking space. I parked my car and sent a text message to pay for the parking. I paid for two hours this time, just in case.

While walking to the cafe, all the crosswalks turned green as I approached them. The weather was on the hotter side, so I was glad for the quick change. Today was turning out to be a great day. I crossed the last pedestrian crossing and walked into the cafe.

I didn't spot Khalid as I made a scan of the tables. The barista enthusiastically greeted me as I passed by, and I waved hello. I sat at the exact same table we'd been sitting at before, effectively making it our regular.

I checked my phone and saw that it was five minutes past noon. There was also a message from my mom asking if I was having iftar at our place or my aunt's. I sent her back a response and put my phone away.

As I waited for Khalid, I glanced around the

cafe. It was practically empty. The few people who were there were either on their laptops or with someone else, probably having their own meetings. I sat there staring out the window and thought about what more I needed to do for my dissertation.

After a while, I pulled out my phone and checked the time. Fifteen minutes had passed. I opened the message he sent the previous night and made sure that I had the date right. It was strange for Khalid to be late. It was even stranger that he didn't notify me about it. I decided to wait another five minutes before checking in with him.

I opened Khalid's message and was typing a follow-up message when I saw Khalid rush in through the front doors. His hair looked like he ran his hand through it multiple times, his tie was loose, and his usually pristine shirt was wrinkled.

He didn't even bother to look around the cafe. He turned in my direction and power walked to the table. See, our regular.

Khalid sat with a breathless, "Sorry I'm late." His knee was shaking under the table. He seemed tense.

"It's fine. But are you alright? You look like you're about to run a marathon or ran a marathon." I was going for jokey, but he only got more tense. He ran a hand through his hair and blew out a very long breath.

"Noor," he stopped abruptly. He wasn't making eye contact with me either. There was definitely something wrong. I tried to catch his eye, but he looked lost in thought. His phone received a notification, and he grabbed it so fast I thought I would get whiplash just watching him reach for it.

Khalid proceeded to stare at his phone for a good couple of minutes before he started brutally typing something in. I waited patiently. He seemed like he needed a minute, maybe a couple hundred.

Finally, he put down his phone—more like slammed it—and let out a deep sigh as he massaged his temples. He sighed again before he looked at me and said, "We have a problem."

He didn't say anything else after that, so I prompted him along.

"What's the problem?" I asked slowly. He seemed hesitant to answer.

"It's the company."

My heart nearly stopped beating. What could possibly be wrong with my company? It wasn't even a company yet.

Khalid continued. "We seemed to have made an error in judgment."

Now, my heart did stop beating. I knew this was too good to be true. I was trying to wrap my head around the flush of devastating disappointment that was filling my blood when Khalid continued again.

"The investment wasn't good. Someone promised a lot more than they could deliver, and now we're paying for it." He stopped and covered his face with his hands.

I was so close to poking him in his pretty eyes. What he was saying wasn't making sense anymore. The investment in the institute was still theoretical; no money was spent. I snapped.

"Khalid, without pausing this time, please tell me exactly what the problem is." There was a smidge of menace in my voice.

He lifted his head and crossed his arms on the table. "A few months ago, the company I worked for made a big investment in a well-established company that wanted to expand its business. We worked with them before, and there weren't any indications that something was amiss, so we made the deal, signed the check. Now, we've got news from that company. They went bankrupt. They were never planning on expanding operations. The money was for covering their debts. It didn't cover even half of it." He said the last sentence so quietly I thought he might have been talking to himself had he not been maintaining eye contact the entire time.

"What does that mean, though? Why are you so distressed?" I asked him.

"It means we've also gone bankrupt, Noor. It means we don't have money. It means I don't have a job. It means we can't invest in your project. I'm so sorry."

His apology was so sincere. Like it came from his soul. I wanted to reassure him that I understood; it wasn't his fault after all, but I was a little busy trying to breathe through the lump in my throat and fighting the tears threatening to fall.

Khalid looked at me, and his face paled.

"Noor, I have a plan," he said quickly.

"What is it?" I asked, hopeful.

"I've created a pretty steady network for myself throughout the years. A list of investors who can help us now. One of them wants to meet with you." He said with a small smile. But I could tell it wasn't reaching his eyes.

"What's the catch?" I asked. His face softened.

"He might say no."

I thought about how tiresome it would be to repeat this all over again—to have to sell my idea and fight for it—and then I thought of the things I'd done to get to this point. I remembered the bridge and the canal. I thought that this moment wasn't the end. I just had to remake and redirect. So, I pulled myself together and let determination straighten my spine.

"I'm all in. Set the meeting," I told Khalid.

A grin split his face, this time reaching his eyes. "I already did. It's today. Right now." And with that, he got up and pocketed his phone. I stared dumbly at him until he gave an urgent "*Yalla.*"

I leaped up from the table and followed him. His long legs meant I was working hard to keep up with his strides. The entire way, Khalid kept up a steady stream of information about the investor and how I might sell the idea to him.

"He's really old school, so he might not see the benefits of starting something brand new. You're going to have to speak to what he does understand, and that's money. Talk up the rental of the facility. I checked your numbers, and they're good. Viable. That's important. Go over everything you remember. Talk about the economic necessity, which, thankfully, the institute has a lot of."

He went on and on without stopping to catch his breath. I absorbed as much of what he was saying while simultaneously going over the budgets and expenditures I had researched. I was nervous about the sudden presentation, but that didn't matter. I had to focus. My future was on the line.

The investor's office was in the building just above the cafe. We took the stairs to the first platform of office buildings. We entered one building and took the elevator up. We stepped off and walked ahead, where there was a glass door. Khalid held it open for me. In front of the door was a grand reception desk. The room was all marble floors and natural light from the generous windows.

"We have an appointment with Mr. Ibrahim," Khalid told the receptionist.

The receptionist smiled and asked for our names. Khalid recited them to him.

"Mr. Saleh! Mr. Ibrahim is waiting for you in his office. Please go straight ahead."

Khalid thanked him and took off on what I assumed was the way to Mr. Ibrahim's office. He didn't ask for directions.

"Do you know Mr. Ibrahim well?"

"I do. He's the one who recommended me to the investment company I work for. *Worked* for. He's been my strongest ally and always took a chance on me, so I'm hoping he'll do the same for you."

"Okay, great. That sounds promising."

We reached the end of the hall, where we came across another pair of glass doors. Inside, I could see a man who looked to be in his late fifties with salt-and-pepper hair slicked back the way I've seen my grandfather wear it in old photos, sitting behind a large oak desk. He spotted us through the glass and enthusiastically waved us in. We walked in and sat in the seats opposite Mr. Ibrahim.

Khalid first greeted Mr. Ibrahim and then relaxed in his chair. I said my hellos and sat ramrod straight in mine. I silently watched Khalid and Mr.

Ibrahim catch up with each other. Mr. Ibrahim seemed like a jovial man. He had an old uncle feeling about him. It helped me relax a little.

Finally, the niceties were finished, and the conversation turned to the reason why we were here.

"So, Noor. Khalid says you have a proposal for me." His eyes settled on me like he was genuinely eager to hear about my idea.

I took a steadying breath and gave my speech. I went over my general idea, then followed with details on construction and expenses, and finally I recounted the pitch I had given Khalid. Throughout the speech, Khalid remained silent, allowing me to express my thoughts.

Mr. Ibrahim's face went from being friendly to blank. I couldn't read what he was thinking. I couldn't get any facial clues from him, so I had no idea if I was talking too much or too little.

When I felt like I had said all that needed to be said, I concluded with a request for an investor and waited. I glanced over at Khalid to read his face the same moment he looked at me. While his face was impassive, his eyes were triumphant.

Khalid then turned to Mr. Ibrahim to ask him what he thought. I thought he might want some time to consider and evaluate, but he gave me a sorry look and said to Khalid, "No."

Fourteen

We walked back to the elevator in silence. After Mr. Ibrahim's very resolute response, Khalid thanked him for his time and was all smiles and reassurances as Mr. Ibrahim explained his reasons. He was such a good-natured person that I couldn't even despise him for his refusal. I gave him my own thanks and left.

Now, waiting for the elevator, the tension was so palpable I could've cut it with a pair of scissors. I looked up at Khalid and grinned.

"All things considered, I think that went well."

All things considered it really *did* go well. Mr. Ibrahim was polite, and while I was heartbroken, I realized he said no because he didn't think it was a suitable investment for him. He didn't say one bad thing about the idea. That was something, at least.

The elevator arrived, and we stepped in. I pressed the button for the ground floor.

"How can you be so positive about this?" Khalid asked.

"It's the perfect time to be positive. Did you think people meant you should be positive when things are going right? What's the use of positivity, then? You have to be positive when things are going wrong. That's how things go right again."

He looked at me for a moment, and I watched as he stood straight and took a deep breath.

"You're right," he said. "And it's time for things to go right again."

The elevator reached the ground floor, and we stepped out into the midday heat. I started walking towards the cafe again, but Khalid went straight for a patch of shade. I followed. When I reached him, he had his phone out and was typing into it.

"This is what we're going to do: we're going to meet with every possible investor I know, and we're going to get your research institute to its development phase. We have four days until the weekend, and then Ghada's deadline is the Friday after. I'm certain we can hook someone by then. It'll be a hectic week. Are you okay with that?"

See, positivity. It gets you places.

"Yes," I told him. I made it this far—there was no point giving up now.

"Great," Khalid said and continued typing.

I assumed he was sending out emails and scheduling appointments. I remembered that his company going bankrupt wasn't just bad for me, it was bad for him, too. Honestly, it was worse for him. He lost his job. I only had an idea to lose.

"Khalid, what about you?" I asked. "You don't have a job anymore. Shouldn't you take this time to look for something new?"

"Don't worry about me." He never broke eye contact with his phone. "This is more important. We have to get you set up."

"But, Khalid, everyone in your company was laid off. That means everyone will be looking for new jobs. You have to start before all the good ones are taken," I urged. He must have noted the panic in my voice. He looked up from his phone and grinned at me.

"But, Noor, we have to be positive."

"Be positive, yes, but also be proactive." He didn't hear me. He just continued using his phone. I tried again. "I won't do it." My voice was embedded with as much severity as I could muster. He gave me a curious look. I crossed my arms. If he was going to be difficult, then so would I. "I won't go to the interviews."

"Noor, I'm doing this for you." He sounded frustrated.

Good. He loved his job. I hated the thought of

him ending up with something he wasn't just as passionate about.

"And I'm doing this for you."

We both stood there, glaring at each other.

Khalid caved first. I could see it in his face before he spoke and grinned at my victory.

"Okay," he said. "I'll look into jobs if you go to the interviews."

"You've got a deal. But you also have to report back to me daily, so I know you're keeping up your end of the bargain."

"Aww, do you care that much about me?" he teased.

I hesitated a second too long.

"Don't flatter yourself," I said, but the damage was done. Khalid just smiled. "Whatever. It's hot. Can we go?" I was desperate to run from that smile.

"Yeah, we can. It is hot. I'll walk you to the car before I head back to the off—" He cut himself off and cringed, realizing he didn't have anywhere he needed to be. "Wow, okay, that's going to get some getting used to. I still need to organize the meetings with the investors, so I guess I'll just work in the cafe."

"Come on, then. I'll walk you to the cafe."

We walked out from under the shade, and I instantly missed the slight coolness it provided. I was going to need a couple of liters of water during iftar tonight to make up for the heat.

"Thank you, by the way. For not giving up," I told Khalid as we headed toward the entrance. He was going out of his way to help me. It literally wasn't his job anymore, but he was still giving me all his time. "I just want you to know that I appreciate everything you're doing."

"I believe in your vision, Noor. So much so that I feel like it's become mine as well." He was quiet for a moment. "And I don't want to let you down." He said it so quietly I thought maybe I wasn't supposed to hear.

It made me smile. "I appreciate it. I appreciate everything," I told him.

We reached the bottom of the stairs, right where the cafe was.

"I'll get something set up for tomorrow. Expect a text from me sometime later today," he said.

I nodded. "Make sure you get a list of available job positions as well. That's your first task. And don't think I'll forget either. By the end of this, I will have my company, and you will have a job."

"You make it sound like a punishment. But okay, I accepted this challenge, and I will uphold my end of the bargain. Prepare to be amazed at how fast I can get a job."

"Were you this confident the first time you were looking for a job?" I asked.

"God, no. I was a nervous wreck at every interview, and I didn't land a job until eight months after graduation." He rubbed his palms together. "But now, I have years of experience and connections. This will be easy."

"Your confidence is borderline cocky, but we probably need some cockiness to help us get through this. It's a good thing you have enough to spare."

He glared at me good-naturedly. I grinned, told him I'd talk to him later, and took off. I turned around to steal one more glance and caught Khalid still standing where I left him with his hands in his pockets. When he saw me turn, he lifted his hand and waved. I could see him smiling from across the road. I waved back and turned to cross the other side of the street.

I walked quickly to the car and shoved my key into the ignition. Fortunately, the entire ordeal had taken less than an hour, so I didn't return to a surprise ticket again. I pulled out of the parking lot and made my way home.

As the roads unfurled before me, mile after mile, I was a mix of emotions. I was disheartened that the research institute was back on pause, sad that Khalid was out of a job, hopeful that we had a plan of action for both of us, nervous about presenting my idea again, and excited at the prospect of achieving what seemed to be impossible. Finding a new investor in four days was stretching it. But I had faith in us.

I reached home and didn't know what to do with myself. I had time until I went to the hospital in the afternoon to see Maha and her new baby. She sent us a text message very early in the morning to let us know that she was officially the mother of a beautiful baby boy. The group chat texted her the whole night with no response. After hours of waiting with no news, she sent us a picture of her holding her son. We didn't get time to speak with her. Understandably. But her reception was starting that afternoon, and we planned on being the first people there. And since we would all be there, it was the perfect time to fill everyone in on yesterday's events.

I could have spent the time revising my dissertation, but I wasn't in the mood for it. I had so much adrenaline after this morning that I wanted to do something. I pulled out my laptop and sat at the dining table. I opened up the business proposal document and started planning. There would be so much that would need to be done if the project went through, and while I put in a lot of detail into the proposal, I could still work on the logistics of running a research facility.

I only stopped working at the sound of my mom closing the door behind her. I got up and kissed her cheek. We sat on the couch and talked about our days. I told her I had a meeting with Khalid but glossed over the part where I found out my institute was doomed and then saved. Her expression changed a little when I said Khalid's name. It was like she was analyzing the situation. Or analyzing me. Then we talked about my aunts and uncles and cousins, and she filled me in on her day at work as a school teacher. It was mostly the same things we talked about over the phone when I was away, but it was so much better being near her.

When it was time to go to the hospital, I left the house to pick up Lamya and Aysha. Hospital parking spots were not easy to find, so it made more sense for us to go in one car.

I picked Lamya up first from the home she lives in with her parents. As soon as she got in the car, she demanded I tell her what happened at yesterday's meeting with Khalid, but I told her she had to wait until Aysha was with us. She agreed and filled me in on her day, but most of the civil engineering lingo went over my head. A couple of minutes later, we were outside Aysha's house. She got in the car and also demanded to know what had happened yesterday. I called Heba, and with Lamya and Aysha in the car listening, I told them everything. Their reactions transformed from patiently listening to amused to shocked to laughing hysterically. By the time we found parking at the hospital, they were all caught up. As far as they were concerned, I had an investor for my research institute. I would rectify that as soon as Maha was with us.

We entered the hospital and went to the gift shop. We spent a good twenty minutes choosing between stuffed animals and baskets of chocolates and fighting over who would get to buy the cuter card. Lamya won. We purchased our goodies and made our way to the maternity ward. I could feel our excitement grow with each step. We'd known Maha since forever, and it was strange to think of her as a mother, even though we had been expecting it for nine months.

In the elevator, we spoke about how strange it was that one of us was married with a child and that the rest of us would eventually follow suit. A silence came over us after that, lost in our own thoughts. It's strange how you can wake up one day, and all of a sudden, the future is your present. I thought I'd have Maha's life by this age. It never dawned on me that plans change and the things you wanted wouldn't happen when you expected them to. I think Heba would agree with me, given that our lives have taken similar trajectories. I could see Lamya or Aysha following this path soon if they wanted it.

The elevator reached the maternity ward, and we turned down the corridor to find room 306. On the door to Maha's room was a sign. A single name was written on it in beautiful Arabic calligraphy, Jasim.

We pushed open the door and started squealing until Maha firmly shushed us, and we realized Jasim was sleeping in her arms. Auntie Nisreen was sitting on the couch and took the gifts we brought. We practically ran to Maha's bed and crowded over her, showering her in hugs and kisses, and did our best not to wake the baby. We were early enough that we had Maha and Jasim all to ourselves.

Fifteen

"Why does he look like a potato."

I smacked Aysha on the back of her head. Lamya leaned over Maha from the other side of the bed and smacked her as well. Both hits meant *you don't tell a new mother that her baby looks like a potato.* Aysha seemed to have gotten the message and corrected herself.

"Sorry. I meant to say he looks like a *beautiful* potato."

I was about to smack her again, but she anticipated my reaction and backed away from my reach, cackling the whole time. Lamya and I glared at Aysha, but Maha was indifferent. She was lovingly looking at her baby and stroking his cheeks.

"He is a beautiful potato, isn't he?" she said without looking up at us.

Lamya and I took our cue and agreed that he

indeed was a beautiful potato. Aysha inched toward the bed and gave us a victorious grin.

We spent the next half hour taking turns holding the baby and listening to Maha recount her experience. Growing up in large families, we all knew other people who had had babies before. Usually, they were older siblings or cousins. So, most of what Maha told us wasn't new, but we listened and were still awed because it doesn't matter how many times you hear a delivery story, the strength and resilience of every single woman who goes through it never ceases to amaze.

Maha finished her story and reclaimed Jasim. I decided then was as best a time as any to make my announcement. I cleared my throat, and three sets of eyes looked at me.

"So," I started off. "I've got some news. I met with Khalid again today, and he told me that his company went bankrupt, and he's out of a job."

The girls exploded in gasps.

Lamya recovered first. "What do you mean bankrupt? What does this mean for you?" she asked. Maha and Aysha were looking at me, waiting for the rest of the story.

"He said that there was a bad investment, and it wiped out the company. As for me, since the company no longer has money, I no longer get my investment. I'm technically back at square one."

"What do you mean 'technically'?" Maha asked.

"Khalid still wants to help. He's going to set up meetings with investors that he knows. We have four days until the end of the week, so hopefully, someone will say yes by then. If not, then I'll have to tell Ghada on Friday that there's no investor, and that'll be it for the institute." As I spoke, I realized I was okay with it. If the research facility didn't happen, I would be okay because I would have done everything possible to make it happen.

"Do you think you'll find someone?" Lamya asked.

"I don't know. I hope so. I'm staying optimistic. I think we just need to find the right person who would be interested in the idea, not so much the money-making scheme. Khalid really was the perfect investor. He's been so kind. He's going above and beyond for it."

Aysha gave me a smug look. "You mean for you."

"What are you talking about?" I asked, genuinely confused.

"You said he's going above and beyond for *it*. I'm saying he's going above and beyond for *you*."

"Don't be ridiculous. It's his job. That's why he did everything he did," I retaliated, but I sensed a hint of untruth in the statement. No, I was being ridiculous. Khalid is just that nice.

"It was his job when he *had* a job. If he's not your investor anymore, there's no reason for him to assist you." She paused and looked absolutely gleeful. Like evil grinning. "Unless he simply *wants* to assist you. Because he cares."

"He cares about the project," I said firmly. "He said so himself. He cares because he cares about it, not me."

"He can say a lot of things, but he probably means something entirely different," Lamya interrupted.

"Even if he is doing it for me, so what? It doesn't mean he's interested. Like I said, he's nice." Now, everyone was looking at me. "Nothing I say is going to convince you otherwise, is it?"

"Nope," Maha, Lamya, and Aysha said simultaneously.

The baby woke up just then and made cooing noises. I went and picked him up.

"You're on my side, aren't you, Jasim? You can be my new partner in crime. My old ones are broken." My phone buzzed in my bag. I handed Jasim to Aysha, who was making grabby hands in my direction. I pulled my phone out and saw that I had a text from Khalid. I involuntarily smiled at my phone. The girls picked up on it like a group of sharks smelling blood.

"Who is that?" Aysha asked.

"Does it start with a K?" Lamya smirked.

I glared at them both before I answered. "It's Khalid."

"What does he want?" Aysha sing-songed.

"If you'd give me two seconds to read it, I'll let you know."

She made a shooing motion with her hands. I gave her one more stern glare before I read the message.

> Hi, Noor. I just wanted to let you know about our next investor meeting. I found someone who is willing to interview you tomorrow at 2pm. I hope that's suitable for you. Please let me know if you're available.

Hi

Tomorrow at 2pm is perfect.

Who am I meeting and where is the meeting going to be at?

> We'll be meeting Ms. Alaa at her office in DIFC. I can meet you in the parking beforehand and we can walk there together.

Oh, you're coming with me. That's great!

> Thought I'd come along for moral support.

Do you mean to babysit me?

> I mean to be there for you.

> Did you know I've lived in Dubai
> almost all my life but this is the most
> I've ever been to DIFC in a one-
> month period.
>
> Actually, It's the most I've been.
> Ever.

I did not know that. DIFC was half
my life.

> Don't worry, we'll get you situated
> there again.

I'm staying positive :)

I could vaguely hear someone calling my name. I was about to type something when a hand appeared in front of my face and snatched the phone away. "Hey!"

Lamya took my phone and was leaning over it with Maha and Aysha, reading my messages.

"That's an invasion of my privacy." I tried to snatch the phone back, but Lamya passed it to Aysha who continued reading my messages, but aloud so the rest could hear. Thank God Auntie Nisreen was out of the room.

"You can't seriously expect us to believe there's nothing happening with these texts?" Maha asked, her one eyebrow raised.

"Actually, I do. Because there's nothing in the texts." I crossed one arm and stretched the other, singling to Aysha to give the phone back. After a five-second stare-down, she finally gave in and handed it back. Khalid didn't respond, so I locked the phone and put it away. Not like locking it would have helped much—they all knew my passcode.

I heard Aysha sigh deeply. I caught her rolling her eyes so hard they practically rolled back into her head. I rolled my own eyes at her dramatic display.

"I give up," she said. "She's going to have to see it on her own."

"Yeah, you're right. We might as well leave it for now. She'll be seeing enough of Khalid as it is." This came from Lamya. Maha nodded. They were talking as if I wasn't in the room.

I would have said something, but Auntie Nisreen came back in, which made everyone suddenly freeze. We all stood very still where we were standing—lying in Maha's case—and watched her take her seat on the sofa again. I think the fact that no one said anything raised her suspicions. Auntie Nisreen was no fool—she raised Maha, after all.

She took one look at us and asked, "What's happening here?"

My mind was working at 300km an hour trying to come up with something that wasn't boy-related. We were taking so long that Auntie Nisreen crossed her arms and raised her eyebrow. That look was pure Maha.

Lamya saved us. She heaved an overly dramatic sigh and said, "Maha wants us to take her out for pizza. Right now. For iftar."

Auntie Nisreen gasped and frowned. Maha turned sharply and glared at Lamya while Aysha and I tried not to laugh. Blaming it on the new mother was perfect since she wouldn't get into that much trouble.

"You know you're not supposed to move yet, hayati," Auntie Nisreen scolded. "You'll be on your feet soon enough." There was something poetic about Auntie Nisreen calling Maha 'her life' when Maha was holding her own life in her arms. Auntie Nisreen went to Maha, fluffed her pillow, and gazed at Jasim. "So, girls, when will it be your turn?"

Lamya, Aysha, and I groaned collectively.

"That's our cue to leave," Aysha said. "If I stay any longer, I might actually catch the baby bug and do something radical like get married. Also, I'm hungry. It's almost time to break fast."

We said goodbye to Auntie Nisreen, Maha, and Jasim and promised we would visit soon after she was settled with the baby at home.

"We want pictures. Lots and lots of pictures," I told Maha as we made our way to the door.

"I don't think I'll be taking pictures of anything

else for a while. Only beautiful potato pictures." We all laughed and closed the door behind us.

We retraced back down the hall.

"I can't believe she's a mom," Lamya said. She spoke quietly, lost in her own thoughts.

"I can. She always did want to be settled. Career, husband, baby. It was in her ten-year plan, remember?" I asked them. We reached the elevator and found it already on our floor. We stepped in and hit the button for the ground floor.

"I kind of wish I had that," Lamya said.

"A baby?" Aysha asked.

"Not just the baby. I wish my life was settled. The future is still so empty. I work for the next fifty years. Okay, great. But what then? What else is there? It might be nice to start a family."

"You can always have that, Lamya," I told her.

Lamya snorted. "With what man? I don't want an arranged marriage."

"Maha did it. And she's really happy," Aysha pointed out.

We reached our level and got off.

"I know, but I don't know."

"You don't have to decide today or tomorrow. Don't worry about the future. It will meet you soon enough. If you wake up one day and decide you're ready, then that's when you decide. If you want to fall in love, we'll find you someone. And if you want an arranged marriage, we'll also help you find someone. As for work, you can always mix it up and quit," I told her. She whipped her face to look at me. I chuckled.

"You were giving great advice up until then," she said.

"Maybe not exactly quit," Aysha said, "but she's got a point. If you're bored at work, you can ask to take on a new project or switch departments. You're a genius engineer. I'm sure they'll understand and be happy to find you something new."

"Yeah, that makes sense actually. I'll talk to my boss about it." She smiled sweetly. "Thank you, guys."

"Anything to put that beautiful smile on your face." I gave her a flirtatious grin, and she laughed.

On the way home, I thought of what we said. Maha seemed to have her life set. She had a job, is married, and now has a child. It was hard to think about my future when the present seemed so uncertain. And I must have been spending too much time on this research proposal because when I tried to imagine my life, Khalid's face popped up.

CHAPTER

Sixteen

The entire family was having iftar at my Auntie Manal's that night, so I dropped Lamya off first since her house was furthest, then Aysha, who's house was closer to my aunt's. We called Heba in the car to fill her in on the news of Khalid's company going bankrupt and what it meant for me. She was as shocked by the events as everyone else had been.

Lamya and Aysha were also quick to tell Heba their theory about Khalid and me. This time, I remained quiet and let them theorize all they wanted. They would see when the time came that nothing was going on. We updated her on Maha, and she told us about her day as a biology doctoral candidate, which was a lot like my life in Massachusetts, running between labs and supervisor meetings and quick coffee breaks.

It's been a while since we were all together like this. There was always either one or two of us missing since Heba and I were studying abroad. I could imagine how Heba feels right now: happy to hear from us but aching because she had to be filled in instead of experiencing it with us. Before she hung up, we told her we loved her and couldn't wait to see her again.

Once Aysha was dropped off, it was a short five minutes to my aunt's house. I was running a little late for iftar, so I expected everyone to already be there and seated at the table, eating. As I pulled up to the house, I recognized the line of cars parked outside. I also noticed a few that I didn't recognize. Ahmed and Mohammed probably had some of their friends over. I had to park by the neighbor's house because of them and noticed an SUV that looked like the one Khalid drove the other day when he dropped Maha off at the hospital. I couldn't be sure if it was his or not—I didn't have the license plate memorized. Ahmed and him were friends, so it was entirely possible that he was here. I didn't want to think too much about it, but my steps hurried a little as I walked through the front gate.

I entered the house and found everyone sitting at the dining table or strewn about the living room on various couches. I gave a general greeting to the room as a whole. There were too many cheeks to kiss during *iftar*. Everyone was accounted for except

Ahmed and Mohammed. A simple inquiry confirmed that they were with their friends in the outside majlis—the extra living room that was situated outside the house. I started loading food on a plate, grabbing a date, and breaking my fast in the process. We didn't have to break our fast with a date, but it was a religious tradition I liked to follow.

Once I had my food, I made my way over to where my sisters, Mona, and Hana were sitting. A lot of my other cousins were around, too, but since the five of us were the closest in age, we tended to stick together.

"How's Maha and the baby?" Hessa asked.

I took a spoonful of food and took my time chewing before I swallowed and answered her.

"They're doing well. Jasim is the cutest thing ever. You're all invited to her place after she's settled with the baby." They seemed really excited about the prospect and started discussing what they would buy for the baby. I took that as my opportunity to eat. Too soon, their conversation ended, and I was interrupted mid-chew.

"How's the institute going, Noor?" Hana asked.

I looked at her in surprise as I realized that I never updated them since the laser tag event. I summarized everything for them and ended it by telling them what Khalid and I planned to do next. They were quiet throughout.

"So, your first meeting is tomorrow?" Sara asked.

"Yup, at two." Assuming I was done explaining, I continued eating. My food was cold, but cold food was just as good at that point.

There was a knock at the door, and the girls who wore the hijab and had taken it off rushed to put it on before calling out for the person to enter. I hadn't taken mine off, too in a rush to break my fast for being late, so I stayed put. The door opened, and in came Ahmed, Mohammed, and their friends. One of whom was Khalid. He noticed me sitting on the couch as soon as he came in. If I had to name his expression, I would have said he was pleasantly surprised. He smiled in my direction and winked. I gave him a quick closed-mouth smile back—seeing as my mouth was full of food—and looked away, but the grins I got from the girls told me they saw it, too. I pretended I didn't notice them and focused intently on my plate. Winks were friendly, right?

When we were all done with our food, we took the deck of cards from the living room and went to Hana's room to play a few rounds. We arranged a blanket and threw some pillows on the floor to create a makeshift picnic space. We quickly headed back to the kitchen and snatched a dallah of chai, a dallah of Arabic gahwa, and an assortment of snacks and pastries. Once we were back in the room, I opened the gahwa and breathed in the strong aroma of the Arabic coffee within. Tea was great, but coffee was life.

We sat on the floor, and I shuffled the cards, then passed them to Mona to deal out. We played two rounds of Hokm before Ahmed burst into the room without knocking.

"You're supposed to knock before you enter a room," Hana told her brother. He ignored her, knelt on our blanket, and started eating our snacks. Mohammed was leaning against the door, a bored expression on his face.

"Please remove your older brother," I said to Mohammed.

"He's not going to leave until you give us the deck of cards."

Ahmed made a confirming noise and continued to inhale our food. He tried to pick up Mona's glass of tea, but she smacked his hand away. We didn't have extra cups, so the drinks were safe at least, but if he stayed any longer, we would be out of food.

"As you can clearly see, we're playing right now. Come back in an hour," Hana told her brothers as she tried to push Ahmed away.

Ahmed swallowed and narrowed his eyes. "You know you're going to be playing for longer than that."

"Probably. Why don't you go buy cards? The store is two minutes away."

"Why should we buy cards when we already have cards?" Ahmed asked.

"Because *we're* using the cards," Hessa told him, speaking slowly as if he were a child who couldn't understand. Ahmed looked at the discarded cards in the middle of our circle. We all saw what was about to happen.

Ahmed went to snatch the cards, and we all moved and started grabbing whatever we could lay our hands on and hiding them under us. Our game was ruined, but the cards were safe. He growled in frustration and tried to move Mona out of the way. This was getting out of hand. I pled with Mohammed one more time, but he was too amused to help at that point and, as a middle child between Ahmed and the girls, had always stayed out of our squabbles. He wasn't going to be any help at all.

A new idea came to me. I picked up my phone as Mona and Ahmed wrestled for the cards.

Please come and remove your
friend from our vicinity.

Why is he there? He said he was
going to get us some cards to play
with.

We have the cards.

And we're not giving it to you.

Then I guess we're at an impasse.

You can buy your own deck!

:)

That was useless. Ahmed pushed Mona backward and was grabbing some of the cards that were under her. He held the cards away from her, but that brought them closer to me, so I snatched what was in his hands.

"Hey! Those are mine."

"No, they're not. They're ours. And since you refuse to go buy your own, I will go buy some more." He whooped as I made the last statement. I cut him off. "But I'm going to take this deck with me as well."

"What? Why?"

He looked so confused I actually wanted to just give him the cards. But I had a point to prove.

"Because this way, it's fair. You want our cards, but you won't replace them for us, so we'll replace them and *then* give you ours." I grinned wickedly. I picked up whatever cards were in front of me, and the girls picked up the rest to pass them to me. Ahmed tried to grab some cards, but there were too many of us. He shot Mohammed a look, but he was now busy with his phone. Once I had all the cards, I got up and exited the room. The entire way out of the house, Ahmed tried to pull the cards from my hands, but I knew his tactics and easily moved my hand out of reach.

He finally gave up as we left the house. The girls followed behind me, and we hopped in Hessa's car. Just like I told Ahmed, the store was two minutes away. It was a small grocery situated by the mosque. We didn't even have to leave the car. We paid exactly two dirhams for the deck and were back at the house in under seven minutes. I walked up to the door of the majlis and knocked. Etiquette matters.

Khalid opened the door. He flashed me a grin, and I couldn't help my returning smile. He was wearing regular black joggers and a black T-shirt. Casual Khalid looked nice. He leaned against the doorframe and stuck his hands in his pocket.

"Who would have thought that seeing you twice in one day would brighten up my night?" he said casually.

I narrowed my eyes at him. "Don't think you can butter me up with pretty words. Here's your deck of cards." I handed him the old deck that we had been using earlier. Some were wrinkled from years of use and in the process of all the snatching.

"I thought you bought new ones." He was looking at the deck of cards as if they had offended him.

"I did. The new pack is for me. I thought since

Ahmed was so eager for *these* cards, I'd let him have it."

Khalid sighed and took the deck from my hands. Ahmed walked up to the door behind him and threw an arm over Khalid's shoulder. He inspected the cards in Khalid's hand.

"Where's the other deck?" Ahmed asked.

I stared. "What other deck?"

"How do you expect us to play Hand with just one deck?"

"You didn't say you wanted two decks. You were happy taking the one deck that we had."

"That's because we only needed one deck then. Now, we want to play Hand, and that needs two decks."

"Too bad. You only have one deck. Play a game that uses one."

"Nope. Where's the new deck you bought?"

I didn't say anything. Ahmed stepped away from Khalid and moved past me to go into the house. I breathed deeply through my nose—he was going after the new cards that were currently with Sara.

Khalid remained quiet through the entire exchange. I was just about to tell him off when he handed me back the old cards.

"Here," he said with a smile. "Just do me a favor and tell Ahmed you snatched them from me."

I beamed and took the cards. "Oh, I like you. He

can keep you. He might still come back for this deck, too, if he's so intent on playing Hand."

"I'll change his mind," Khalid said. I huffed out a laugh.

"For two people who have known each other for as short a time as you two have, you're pretty comfortable with each other," I said.

"It must be a family trait. It's just so easy to be around him. Are you ready for tomorrow?" The sudden switch in topic prevented me from analyzing the first thing he said.

"Yes, I am. I'm staying positive about the whole thing."

He smiled. "Thanks to a certain someone, so am I."

Just then, I heard the sound of the house door slamming. I quickly hid the deck of cards out of Ahmed's line of sight. He charged past and wrapped an arm around Khalid's neck.

"Come on, let me show you how great I am at Hand," Ahmed said. He gave me a triumphant grin before he turned him and Khalid around. Ahmed was going to be sorely disappointed when he found out I had the other deck, and I did not envy Khalid's task of placating him.

As soon as the door closed, I bolted. The girls and I had a game of Hokm to finish.

Seventeen

The next morning, my nerves woke me up bright and early. I tried to go back to sleep, but it was useless. The nerves only intensified in bed. So, I got up, grabbed my laptop to read some articles for my dissertation, highlighted important passages, and took notes. Redirecting my focus helped with the nerves, and by the afternoon, I was in a somewhat calm state of mind.

Khalid and I met in the parking lot. I was one car ahead when I turned into the lot and snagged the first parking space. While Khalid circled the lot, I paid for parking and waited for him in my car. After making a few rounds, he found a spot near me. It looked tight from where I was sitting, so I got out and made my way over to assist him. He rolled his window down as I approached.

"Are you sure you can fit your car here?" I asked.

"Of course, I can," Khalid said with more confidence than the situation warranted.

I stood by and watched as he attempted to reverse his car into the parking space. The spot was really, really small. I said nothing as his car reversed too far to the left. I crossed my arms as his next attempt took his car too far to the right.

"Are you sure you don't need any help?"

He said nothing as he attempted it a third time. I had to knock on his car to warn him that he was about to scratch the car next to him. I went back to his window.

"I told you the space was too small for your car."

Clearly frustrated, he said, "The space would be perfect if this person hadn't parked on the line."

"I can park it," I told him and held his gaze, expecting him to refuse. He caught me by surprise when he agreed, put the car in park, and opened the door. I stepped in after him and readjusted the seats. Khalid had it all the way back, so I had to bring it all the way forward and readjust the position of the car.

This time, when I reversed, the car smoothly fit straight into the parking space. I put up the window, turned off the ignition, and went to open the door when I realized I was stuck. The space was really, really tiny. I couldn't open the door. I signaled to Khalid to wait before I jumped over the seats to reach the trunk. I was fiddling with the key, trying to locate the button to open the trunk, when Khalid opened the door from the outside.

"Thanks," I told him.

"Don't mention it."

I hopped out of the trunk, and Khalid closed it behind me.

"Don't forget to pay your parking."

"I did while you were acrobat-ing out the car."

"So, tell me some more about Ms. Alaa. Any pointers?"

"I actually don't know much about her. I've met her a few times, and she was always talking about new and exciting things she was investing in, so I thought this might be up her alley."

"So, it'll be a hit or miss with her?"

"Pretty much. I thought it might be worth a try."

We reached the crosswalk, and I pushed the button.

"Well, here goes nothing then." I turned to him while we waited. "How's the job hunting going? Did you find a list of positions?"

The light turned green, and we began making our way across the street. A group of people in suits were walking toward us, one of them was talking on the phone and not paying attention to the people in front of him. Everyone was dodging out of this way. He charged ahead while looking at the ground, his phone glued to his ear. I didn't spot him soon enough, and just as I thought he'd bump my arm, Khalid wrapped an arm around me and moved us both to the right, avoiding the man altogether. His arm disappeared as fast as it had materialized.

"Thank you," I told him appreciatively.

"It's no problem. As for work, I spent most of yesterday afternoon calling some contacts and asking if they had anything available. I've got a couple of interviews scheduled for next week." He said it proudly, and I couldn't help feeling proud of him, too. He worked hard to get to where he is. "And you were right," he continued. "Apparently a lot of people from my old company were calling for work, too. If I had waited, all the positions would have been taken by next week. So, thank you."

"You're welcome. You can buy me a coffee once you're officially hired."

"If that's the case, then you have to buy me a coffee when you're officially a CEO."

"You've got a deal, my friend." I got quiet as we waited for the elevator. My breaths were coming shorter and faster, and I kept repeating the pitch I had ingrained in my memory, too scared that I'd forget if I didn't go over it one more time. With each rejection I'd gotten, it started to feel like maybe this crazy idea wasn't ever meant to be.

Khalid bumped into my shoulder, and I looked up at him.

"Don't be nervous," he said with a smile. I tried to laugh, but it came out broken.

"How can you tell?"

"It's the scary quiet. I can tell you're in your head. Just remember, this is one person's opinion."

I took a deep breath as the elevator arrived and we stepped in.

"You're right. There's just so much and nothing at stake. It's kind of hard juggling between being excited for it to happen and neutral so I don't get disappointed again."

The elevator slowly made its ascent.

"I'm sorry I did that to you," he murmured. I could tell he meant it.

"Khalid, it's not your fault your company went bankrupt. You couldn't have known what was going to happen. I don't blame you." I could see the relief wash over his face. I poked his side. "Smile," I ordered.

"Yes, ma'am."

We reached our floor and stepped off. Like last time, Khalid approached reception and informed the receptionist who we were there to meet. The receptionist smiled politely and told us to head back to the office. As we rounded the corner, I went over some points in my head, preparing myself one last time for the pitch.

This office, much like the last one, had walls made of glass so we could easily see inside. Khalid knocked on the glass, and the woman inside ushered us in. The first thing I noticed was how tidy her office was. Everything was aligned, so much so that I wondered if she used a ruler to straighten everything. Her desk only contained a pen and a single file on it. The file was open on the first page, and I noticed the familiar titles and subtitles—it was my proposal. Khalid must have sent it to her to take a look at.

We sat and went through the pleasantries and introductions. Ms. Alaa was nice enough, but she was more straight-to-the-point than Mr. Ibrahim was. Her hair was shoulder length and slicked back, and she wore a sharp black suit that looked like it was tailored to fit her.

"Well, Noor, I'm ready when you are," she said as she settled with her hands folded on the table in front of her.

"Okay. I want to start a research institute that will carry out advanced scientific investigations but will primarily be used as a way for undergrad and graduate scientists to gain the practical skills they will need to carry out their own research someday.

It will be fully equipped for principal investigators to perform their studies. This institute will be a way for scientific research to enter the region. A wide variety of scientific research. And it will be accessible to the inexperienced and experienced alike. Students can intern, while PhD holders can mentor. It will be a hub for development and scientific learning.

"I'm also aware of the need for revenue to be generated. Therefore, I propose that sections of the lab space be rented out to companies that could use the space to carry out their own tests, such as pharmaceutical companies. I've already contacted—"

Ms. Alaa raised a hand to stop me.

"I'm sorry to interrupt you, Noor. I can see that you have a lot of passion for what you think is a brilliant idea. However, I don't agree. Your idea is rushed and, frankly, improbable. How much revenue do you truly believe you can generate from this? I've seen your proposal, and while it is well-written, it docs not promote the assurance I need to venture into this. Sometimes, dreams are meant to remain fantasies. This is one of those times. Khalid, I heard about your company, and I'm sorry for that, too. But maybe what you should be focusing on now is finding a new job and not entertaining this illusion."

Her words were so sharp they could have cut through stone. I knew she might say no, but to tear apart months of work was a painful slap in the face. I kind of would have preferred a slap in the face compared to this. I quietly thanked her for her time and stood. I expected Khalid to follow, but he remained seated and silent. I was about to nudge him when he spoke.

"With all due respect, Ms. Alaa, I think you're wrong. I can understand the risks you would be taking in venturing into this, and I can understand your reluctance, but I can't, and I won't understand your disrespect." He got up. "I expected more from you."

Ms. Alaa was stunned into silence. Khalid turned around and marched out. I spared her one last glance before I hurried after him. I didn't have to go far. He was waiting for me just out of sight of Ms. Alaa's office. As I reached him, he started off again towards the elevator.

"That was the most amazing putdown I've ever seen," I told him.

"You're not upset?" he asked, concern etched on his face.

"A little, but what you said back there..." I faltered. How could I explain to him how much it meant to me that he believed in this idea strongly enough to go against someone highly esteemed in his line of work?

We reached the elevator.

"Listen, Noor. Just in case anything of what she

just said got to you, you have to know that your idea actually is brilliant and deserves to be recognized. I saw it, Ghada saw it, Mr. Ibrahim saw it, and I know you see it. So, I truly hope you haven't changed your mind."

We reached the ground level and walked out of the building and back to the parking lot.

"What she said, it hurt. But I'm also not convinced by what she said. If anything, I'm more determined to see it through, if only to prove her wrong." I pushed the button for the crosswalk and flashed him a smile. "If you weren't here, I probably would have been a lot less confident right now. Knowing you're just as sure as I am is immensely reassuring. I couldn't have asked for a better business partner." He kept his eyes ahead of him, but I caught a shy smile.

We reached my car. I leaned against the hood, and Khalid did the same moments later. We stood in comfortable silence, watching the other cars roam the parking lot.

"Tell me about the next meeting. Who's the investor?"

"It's in Abu Dhabi. Tomorrow." He turned to ask me, "Is that okay?" I nodded my confirmation. "The investor is a friend of mine, Hashim. He has your proposal and seems keen on meeting you. That's already a good sign. But he's only junior-level. That means he'll have to take the idea and pitch it to his bosses. I don't know any of them, but he thinks they'll go for it."

I looked at him and smiled. "Stay positive."

"Until the very end." He smiled back.

I would go and give it a hundred percent. I owed myself that much.

Eighteen

Khalid called me the next day after the noonday prayer to let me know he was outside my house. It didn't make sense to drive separately, so we would be going together. It would take almost a little over an hour to get there and the same amount of time back.

My parents had asked me yesterday what I was spending my days doing while they were at work. I explained that I had business meetings that I needed to attend, but I didn't tell them the nature of said meetings or their outcomes. When my dad asked about the 'investor,' I gave him Khalid's name and told him and my mom about our planned trip to Abu Dhabi. They looked skeptical. Technically, I shouldn't be out alone with a man, especially not in his car.

A lot of parents would have put their foot down,

but I explained it was a necessary trip for the business, so they gave in. I think my mom was just happy that I wasn't driving the distance to the capital on my own. My dad moved on to asking details about the next steps for my institute, and I told him I wouldn't have any more details until my meeting with Ghada on Friday. Which was true, either I had a new investor, and we moved on to the next phase, or I didn't, and that would be the end of it.

Now, I slipped my shoes on and went to meet Khalid outside.

"Hey," I greeted him. I shut the door and buckled my seat belt.

"Hi," he said. The way he said it had me scanning his face. He didn't look well, and he sounded tired.

"Are you okay?" I asked. "You're pale."

"I don't feel a hundred percent, but I'm okay," he tried to reassure me. He was concentrating too hard on the road. The navigation map was opened on his phone, and the estimated time of arrival was just one hour and twenty minutes.

I examined his face again. "If you need help driving at any point, pull over. Okay?"

"Thank you. I should be fine, but thank you."

I could tell from his tone that he did appreciate it. We left my neighborhood and were now on

Sheikh Zayed Road, the main highway that would take us straight to the capital of the UAE.

Given Khalid's current health, I thought it would be better to stay quiet and let him focus on the road. But as I sat next to him, I realized I didn't know a lot about his life outside of work. I was suddenly very curious.

"Are you an only child?" I asked into the quiet.

"No. I have four older sisters. They're all married and have kids of their own."

"You're an uncle?" The thought of Khalid playing with his little nieces and nephews made me feel all warm inside.

"An uncle to ten nieces and nephews." He was smiling as he said it, and it made me smile.

"Gatherings must be crazy."

"They are, but I wouldn't have it any other way."

"And four older sisters? What's that like?"

"It's like having five mothers. Five homes. They would do anything for me."

"I get that protectiveness. I would do anything for my sisters."

"Are you the oldest then? You all look about the same age."

"I am the oldest. Sara is twenty-one, and Hessa is twenty." As I was speaking, I noticed the car slowing down. There was no congestion ahead of us. I turned to ask Khalid what was wrong when he signaled right.

He was pulling the car over.

"I feel dizzy," he said, his words slurring a little. He stopped on the right shoulder of the highway and turned on his hazard signal. He leaned his head on the headrest and closed his eyes.

I gave him a moment to clear his head.

"Are you going to faint?"

"I hope not." His words were still slurring.

"Can you switch seats with me?"

"I think so." He unbuckled his seatbelt, his movements slow and unsure.

"Here, just jump over," I said as I unbuckled my own seatbelt and stepped out of the car.

When I reached the driver's side, Khalid was already settled in the passenger seat. I adjusted my seat and merged back on the highway. Khalid rested his head on the window, his eyes closed once more.

Ten minutes later, I glanced at him and saw that his face was still pale. "I think you need to break your fast," I told him.

He opened his eyes, blinking them a couple of times.

"I think I have something." He reached into the center console and pulled out a chocolate bar. He unwrapped it and took a small bite.

"Eat more. I'll pull over at the next gas station, and we can get you some energy bars."

He listened and ate the whole thing. By the time we reached the gas station, his color was back, and he was more lucid. I parked the car.

"I'll go get you some things."

"I'll come with you."

"You can sit and rest."

"I have an hour and a half to rest." He unbuckled but stayed seated in the car. His body angled so that he was looking straight at me. He was waiting for my permission.

I heaved an exaggerated sigh.

"Come on."

Khalid grinned and opened the car so quickly like he wanted to get out before I could change my mind. I chuckled and followed him into the convenience store. I picked up a basket and roamed the aisles. The store wasn't big—the aisles reached my shoulder—but I still managed to lose Khalid. I picked up some energy bars, two bottles of water to keep him hydrated, and a light sandwich from the cold food section.

I didn't know what was wrong with Khalid, but I picked up some cold medicine just in case he had come down with something. I turned down the next aisle and came face-to-face with Khalid in the candy section. The sight was so comical I burst out laughing. He had an arm full of different gummy bears, two large energy drink cans, a pack of chips between his teeth, and one hand stretched out to grab something else off the shelf. He swung his head around when he heard my laugh and looked for all the world like a deer caught in headlights.

"What are you doing?" I asked, approaching him. He tried to smile, but the chips were in his way. He grabbed the candy bar off the shelf and strode toward me, dumping his junk food in my basket.

"I'm glad one of us thought of grabbing a basket." He took the basket from my hand and made his way over to the cashier. I eyed his candy haul as he unloaded them from the basket. I remembered the chocolate bar that he kept in his car. It made a lot of sense.

"So, you have a sweet tooth?" I teased.

"I have a sweet everything. The more the sugar, the better."

"How much sugar do you put in your tea?"

"How big is the cup?"

"Regular teacup."

"Three and a half if it's the tiny teaspoon. Two if it's the bigger teaspoon."

"Khalid, habibi, I fear for your health."

He chuckled. "Don't worry. I don't indulge that much. Except for tea. Tea is an exception. Tea is always an exception." He reached for the items I selected for him. He held up the energy bar and scrunched his face at it, eyeing me as if I had offended his mother.

"You're sick. You need energy," I explained. He reluctantly gave it to the cashier.

"What about you? How do you take your tea?" he asked.

"Black."

"What about coffee?"

"Black."

He scrunched his face again. The cashier told us the total, and Khalid gave me a look before he pulled out his wallet and paid. Back at the car, he headed for the driver's side. I stepped in front of him and gave *him* a look. He chuckled and headed for the passenger side.

I drove out of the gas station.

"Water, sandwich, energy bar. In that order. Then you can have junk food." He did as I said without complaints, and after he finished off another chocolate bar, he laid his head back and promptly fell asleep.

The rest of the drive was uneventful. I drove in silence, allowing Khalid to rest before the meeting. He slept so soundly. It wasn't unlike when he was awake. He had a calm, soothing presence. It spoke of stability, strength, and reassurance. He made you feel grounded. That might have been why my boisterous, energetic cousin took to him so well.

An hour later, I crossed the Sheikh Zayed Bridge that linked the mainland to Abu Dhabi's main island. I had driven to Abu Dhabi a few times before—it's just one straight road until you get into the city—but I had to use the map app to navigate through the city. It was another fifteen minutes before I pulled up into the parking lot of a coffee shop in the Al Bateen area, which, according to the navigation app, was my destination.

Khalid stirred just as I put the car in park. We were half an hour early.

"We're here?" he asked groggily.

"We're here," I confirmed. "How are you feeling?" He took a moment to analyze himself. I did the same, examining his face. He definitely had his color back, and his eyes seemed more focused. All good signs.

"I feel better. Not lightheaded, not dizzy. I must not have eaten enough yesterday."

I grabbed the bag with snacks and pulled out another energy bar and a bottle of water.

"Here, have some more. I'll try to catch you if you faint, but I can't promise I'll be able to hold us both up. Better to just make sure you won't actually faint." I grinned as I handed him the items and he chuckled before finishing them off.

"Do I have any crumbs on my face?" he asked once he was done. I inspected his face carefully. A little too carefully if I was being honest with myself.

"Nope," I said a beat too slow. "You're all good." I pretended nothing unusual happened and looked down at my own phone. There were a couple of new messages from Maha, most of which were pictures of Jasim. I smiled at mine and responded with compliments and lots of emojis.

Out of the corner of my eye, I could see Khalid staring at me.

"Who are you talking to?" he asked.

I looked at him and found that he was trying to be neutral, but I heard the curiosity in his voice and could see it in his face.

"Jasim," I told him and went back to sending heart-eye emojis to Maha.

"Who's Jasim?" I was tempted to continue the charade for longer, but my need to show him Jasim's pictures won out. I flipped my phone around and showed him the most recent picture Maha sent of Jasim asleep, swaddled in a blanket.

Khalid grinned from ear to ear as he took my phone and peered more closely at it.

"Is this Maha's son?" he asked. His face was a study in excitement.

"It is."

"Do you have more pictures?"

We spent the next ten minutes going through all the pictures Maha had sent me of Jasim. Khalid spent a good amount of time on each picture, complimenting and praising Jasim as if the baby had been born with a degree. It was adorable. When we'd gone through most of the pictures,

Khalid handed me back my phone and checked his watch. It was time to go.

A thought occurred to me.

"Do you have any meetings planned for us tomorrow?"

He looked away and took a deep breath before looking back at me.

"No," he said. "I couldn't find anyone else."

"So, this is it? One last shot?" Khalid nodded gravely. I shook off the ball of nervous energy that dropped into my stomach and said, "We better make it count, then."

CHAPTER

Nineteen

We entered the coffee shop on the sixth floor of an office building. Khalid looked around, searching for his friend. The casual setting and the fact that Hashim was a junior investor at his company made me feel a lot more relaxed than the previous two meetings had. Khalid must have spotted Hashim because we started weaving our way between tables, moving to one in the back of the coffee shop. A man was sitting at the table with his laptop open in front of him.

"Hashim," Khalid greeted him enthusiastically. Hashim stood and hugged Khalid. When they pulled apart, Hashim regarded me and nodded a greeting.

"Noor, I presume?" he asked, smiling warmly.

"That's me." I instantly felt comfortable.

Once we'd all settled in, Hashim asked how the drive was.

"I felt lightheaded at the beginning of the trip and had to pull over," Khalid said, "I ended up having to break my fast."

Hashim looked concerned now. "Are you okay? Do you need me to get you something?" Before waiting for a response, he made to stand, but Khalid put a hand on his arm.

"No, habibi, I'm fine. Thank you. I feel much better now. I think I was dehydrated. Noor drove us to a gas station, and I picked up some snacks." Hashim gave Khalid a blank stare.

"I sincerely hope you ate something other than chocolate and Haribo."

I had to hide my laugh behind my hand. Khalid had the decency to look abashed.

"That's what he would have done had I not put a couple of healthier options in the basket," I told Hashim. We both turned to Khalid and gave him a knowing look.

"Whatever," he mumbled. "Can we talk about Noor instead?"

Hashim chuckled and looked in my direction.

"I'm sorry for doing this here, but I thought it would be better than fitting us in my cubicle," he chuckled. "I already looked over your proposal, and I can tell you I'd be delighted to back you on this."

"Really? That's great!" I beamed and felt myself relax further.

"Thank you, Hashim. That means a lot to us," Khalid added. Hashim glanced at his friend briefly with an amused look, but it passed quickly.

"It's my pleasure. I just have some questions to make sure I have a full understanding of what you want."

I straightened. "Of course, ask me anything."

We spent the next hour answering Hashim's questions. It was more of a conversation than anything, and I appreciated it. I explained my primary objective for the institute, and Hashim seemed to recognize its importance as well. He wasn't as passionate about it as Khalid was, but he saw the potential just as keenly. It was honestly a relief. Out of all the investors so far, Hashim seemed to get it the most.

"What do you think our success rate with your bosses would be?" I asked.

"They haven't turned down an idea I've pitched so far, so I'd say there's a pretty high success rate."

I smiled, even though I didn't know how much I could trust his confidence.

"But do you think they're the kind of people who would take this kind of risk? It's pretty high profile," Khalid said. "The ones you usually propose are small-scale."

"Don't worry about that. I can persuade them."

"That's all the questions I've got," I said.

"I think I'm good, too."

Khalid nodded. "We really appreciate you helping out, Hashim."

"You know, you two aren't business partners, but you use 'we' and 'our' a lot. What's that about?"

Khalid was about to speak, but I beat him to it.

"Khalid was supposed to be my original investor. We learned that we were both very passionate about this project and were excited to see it come to fruition. When Khalid's company went bankrupt, it was a blow to both of us—not just because he lost his job and I no longer had an investor, but because we realized we couldn't be a team anymore. So, when Khalid came up with the notion to find a new investor through his contacts, it was what we both needed to push ourselves through the nightmare that had happened. We may no longer be business partners, but we've become survival partners. We're here to make sure the other comes out of this better and stronger." I looked at Khalid. "And I couldn't have asked for a better partner."

He smiled, then said, "I couldn't agree more."

We both looked at Hashim.

"I, for one, am thrilled to join this partnership," he said.

"I can't wait to make this official," I told him.

"I've heard everything I needed to hear. Let me get back to the office and run this by my bosses. I have a meeting scheduled with them soon, so you'll probably hear back from me fairly quickly. I know from Khalid that time is of the essence. I'll definitely give you a call by tomorrow, if not today itself."

I was feeling a lot more hopeful as we thanked Hashim and said our goodbyes. Before we left the table, however, Hashim asked to speak with Khalid for a minute. I excused myself and stood by the door. I watched them speak from where I was.

I couldn't make out the words, but I could tell that Hashim was teasing Khalid about something. You couldn't mistake his grin and Khalid's head-shaking in response. Khalid then glanced in my direction with a smile before turning back to Hashim. They wrapped up quickly and made their way over to where I was. As they neared, I opened the door and exited the coffee shop, walking toward the parking lot. They caught up, and we walked together.

"This is me," Hashim said when we passed by a black sedan.

"Thank you again for meeting with us, Hashim. Truly," I replied.

"It's been my pleasure. I was interested in your idea before, but now that I've met with you, I'm excited to get started. This will be great for the region."

I was happy to hear him say so. Walking away from Hashim and the hopes and dreams he now carried with him was one of the hardest things I had to do. I wanted to follow him to his office and hear first-hand what his bosses had to say. Instead, I followed Khalid to his car.

"Do you feel well enough to drive?" I asked. "My leg cramped a little on the way here."

"Of course."

I handed him the keys. Khalid set the navigation setting to my house and pulled out of the parking area.

"We never finished our conversation from earlier," he said. His gaze trained forward, and his fingers tapping a rhythm on the steering wheel.

The movement captured my attention as I asked, "Which conversation?"

"The getting to know each other conversation. I'm going to need to know more about my survival partner." He grinned, but his eyes were serious.

Now, I was the one looking away, my fingers twisting together in my lap. There was more behind his request. A question behind the question. And just like with the proposal I drafted all those months ago, I decided to take the leap and provide an answer within an answer.

I looked back at his profile. "What do you want to know?"

He quickly glanced at me, taking his eyes off the road for less than a second as he said, "Everything."

So, we spent the rest of our trip home learning about each other's lives until that point. We talked about the schools we went to, the people we knew, the career decisions we made, and the things we liked to do. I didn't ask about everything—it was too soon for that—but I could tell he was a good person. He had a good soul. Khalid was telling me about an incident involving a wild goat in the mountains of Ras Al Khaimah when he got an incoming call. My heart stopped, assuming it was Hashim before I read the name—Ahmed.

Khalid put him on speakerphone.

"Hey."

"What are you doing tonight?" my cousin asked without preamble.

"I'm having iftar with my family tonight, but my schedule is clear for later."

"Good, keep it free. I'll pick you up at ten."

"Do you want me to wear something pretty?" Khalid asked. I couldn't stop my snort.

"Who's that?"

"It's Noor," I answered.

"Why are you with Khalid?" Ahmed asked me with lazy curiosity that might have been a cover for suspicion.

"We had a meeting in Abu Dhabi."

"Oh, right. I forgot you two were working together. How's the business going?"

"It's going," I answered. Knowing Ahmed, that would be enough for him.

"What does that mean?" he asked.

I was taken aback. Ahmed never asked for more details.

"It means we're working on getting the project off the ground." It wasn't the truth, but it was close enough.

"That's cool. I'm proud of you, kid."

That left me speechless. The statement was way too sentimental to be coming from my cousin. I stumbled through a reply.

"Thank you, Ahmed. That means a lot. And I'm only three years younger than you."

"Yeah, like I said—kid."

I rolled my eyes. I looked over and saw Khalid silently laughing.

"Khalid, we're going to a tent tonight. So, yes, wear something pretty." With that, Ahmed hung up.

"I'm not the kid, he is," I said indignantly.

"I don't disagree with you."

I was about to say something when my phone rang. I glanced at the screen and saw the call was from an unknown number. I didn't answer strange numbers as a rule and put it on silent before remembering that it might be Hashim. I read the number to Khalid, who confirmed that it was Hashim's number. I took a steadying breath and answered, putting the call on speakerphone.

"Hello?"

"Hi, Noor. This is Hashim."

"Hi, Hashim. I have Khalid on speakerphone with me."

"That's perfect."

The line went quiet for a second. I cast a worried look at Khalid.

"So, listen—" That was all the confirmation I needed, "—I talked to my bosses. I'm sorry, guys. They're just not into it. They're worried about the risks. I tried to tell them about the companies that you were already in contact with, Noor, but they don't think it's enough of a guarantee. I'm so sorry."

I knew it was a long shot. Ever since I started drafting the idea, I knew there was a very high chance that all I would end up with was a proposal.

"Thank you for trying, Hashim. I understand that the project has too many risks."

"It would have been an honor to launch this with you. If you have any other business schemes up your sleeves, bring them to me. You have a brilliant mind, and I look forward to what you'll come up with next."

I grinned at the compliment as I expressed my

gratitude and hung up the phone. Khalid didn't say anything, and I didn't think I could face his disappointment right then. I looked out the window, watching the other cars drive by as I wrangled the emotions storming inside. This was the end of the road. I put my best self forward and chased this dream farther than I thought I could, and it wasn't all for nothing. This was still one of the best Ramadans ever. I found out that my idea held some merit, I discovered the vast amount of faith the people in my support system had for me, and I made a new friend, maybe more, in Khalid. All in all, I gained more than I lost, which was good enough for me.

I still believed a new research institute would make a great addition to scientific learning in the region, but maybe it was an idea that needed to wait for its moment to shine. New investors will come up in a few years, and I'll be there to greet them with my proposal. Until then, I had a PhD to finish.

A few moments later, Khalid exited off the highway. I was familiar with the exit, but I didn't know why he exited. We were nowhere near Dubai yet.

"Where are we going?" I asked him.

"My favorite place."

Twenty

Fifteen minutes later, we passed by a sign that said Jubail Mangrove Park. I'd heard of the place but never been to it myself. Khalid parked the car, and we got out, making our way to what looked like a boardwalk. I followed behind Khalid as I observed the scenery. I could see why this was Khalid's favorite place—it was gorgeous. The boardwalk cut a natural path around and between the mangroves in the vicinity, the sky was clear enough that there was a blue backdrop to all the green, and the water reflected was clear enough that we could see the sediments beneath the mangroves. The place was magical.

Khalid set a leisurely pace. There weren't many people around at this time and the quiet added to the serenity of it all. It was warm today, but there was a slight breeze, which meant it wasn't back-dripping-in-sweat hot. If it looked this great in the hazy summer air, it must be picturesque during the cooler winter months.

Signs along the boardwalk let us know there were different trails. Khalid followed the one with the shortest path. We walked in silence, soaking in the landscape. The boardwalk curved around a mangrove cluster, and a platform appeared. On the map, they called it a floating platform. It was an extension of the boardwalk that jutted out into the water and had no railings. It left you standing right at the edge. One step, and you'd be in the water. I walked all the way to the edge and stared out at the scenery. Khalid walked up to stand beside me.

The silence between us was usually the most natural thing in the world, but this time, it was loaded with tension. I hated it. I was about to say something, anything to lighten the mood when he spoke.

"I'm sorry I disappointed you."

I was shocked by the pain in his voice. All this time, he was silent, and it was because he thought he disappointed *me*. I didn't even know how he could assume I was disappointed in him.

"Khalid, look at me." He did. "I'm not disappointed in you. At all. How could I be? You're the one who made any of this possible. You knew I didn't have the financial factor yet, but you gave me the opportunity to find it. And you could have easily sent me an email letting me know about the situation with your company and be done with me. But you didn't. You told me in person, and I saw how distressed you were. You cared. You cared enough to try to find me another investor. You used contacts that you could have just used for yourself. I could never be disappointed in you. I'm grateful. For your time, for your help, for you."

I held his gaze the entire time, willing him to understand that I meant every word. It spoke volumes of his selflessness that he still didn't think he'd done enough after everything he did. He looked out at the water and put his hands in his pockets. I tried one more time. "Your efforts are recognized, acknowledged, and gratefully received."

I watched as he took a deep breath. He turned back to me and smiled, at first shyly and then brightly.

"Why is it that I crave your honesty?" he asked.

"Probably because I always end up saying nice things about you."

"I can't deny that."

"Come on. Let's see the rest of the park before we leave."

We continued our walk along the path, our footsteps lighter than before.

"So, what's next?" he asked.

"We talk to Ghada on Friday. Tell her what

happened. And then it's just a few days until Eid and a few days more until I leave."

"You'll be gone for a year?"

"No, six months. I'm almost done with my dissertation. It's just reviews and extra lab tests to confirm results from now on. And my final examination, of course."

"And then what?"

"And then I'm back here. Hopefully, the five years of experience I have will land me a research position at a university or even at one of the research centers. I'll have to start applying from now."

"If I knew anyone in the research field, I would have helped you out."

"I know. That seems to be all you do—helping me. I hate that all I've managed to do for you is be there when you lost your job." I couldn't look at him as I said it. I felt so useless.

"Being on this journey with you has been enough. Watching your determination grow in the face of the constant let-downs has been an inspiration. I know a lot of people who only achieved their goals because they had someone hand it to them. You don't just go after your goals; you sprint towards them. I've always believed that one of the best ways to improve as a person is to surround yourself with people you want to learn from. You've become one of those people for me. So don't cut yourself short. Okay?"

I smiled at him. "Okay."

"Besides, you forced me to start looking for a job, and because of you, I've got two interviews next week."

"I hope you get offers from both, and they end up fighting over you. Are they both investor positions?" I asked.

"One is. The other one is a financial consultant position. I'm actually hoping I'll get that one. I've recently been motivated to learn something new." His mouth quirked up in a half grin.

"Then I hope you get that one." I wanted him to get it. He deserved it. He was a good person, and good people deserve good things. "I'll pray for you tonight," I added. It took me a couple of steps before I realized Khalid wasn't next to me. I turned around and found him standing in the middle of the boardwalk with his hands in his pockets. "What is it?"

"You really don't make things easy, do you?"

"What do you mean?" I had no idea what he was going on about.

He chuckled. "Nothing. Come on, let's go. We have to leave now if we're going to make it back by sundown."

We looped back around to the parking lot and got

in the car. Khalid asked me about my dissertation, and I gave him the short version that I usually reserved for people without a background in biology. He wasn't happy with it. I spent the whole trip explaining it all to him, or as much of the four years as I could tell him in an hour's drive, and answering all his questions.

An hour before sunset, Khalid pulled up in front of my house.

"I'll see you Friday," I said.

"Shall I pick you up?"

"No, it's okay. I'll drive. I only have a week before I'm back to walking and public transportation."

"Is it that bad?" he asked.

"Not really. But I miss driving when I'm there."

"Then you should definitely drive yourself. I'll see you in Ghada's office on Friday."

We said goodbye, and I walked into my house. I found my parents and siblings in the kitchen, preparing food for iftar.

"How was Abu Dhabi?" my dad asked.

"Not so great, Baba."

They must have heard the despondency in my voice because everyone stopped what they were doing and watched me. It was time to tell them. I recapped what had been going on. Sara and Hessa already knew about the meetings, so they remained quiet and listened as I explained that part. I told them everything, detailing each meeting with Mr.

Ibrahim and Alaa and what was said. No one interrupted me. Finally, I reached today's meeting.

"On the way back from Abu Dhabi, Hashim called. He said his bosses were not going to back the project. So, that's it." It was hard to keep down the bitter taste of failure that was creeping up my throat.

Tears were stinging my eyes, and I looked down to hide them. It was easy to see the bright side with Khalid because he was there and saw how hard I fought. But my family is only hearing how I couldn't convince anyone to support my idea. I felt a pair of arms around me and inhaled my mom's familiar scent. Then, another two pairs, as my sisters joined in. And then my dad, who wrapped his arms around all of us and squeezed. Tears slid down my face one by one. Slowly at first, but then I took in a breath, and they rushed out with my exhale until I was sobbing.

With every tear, I let go of a little piece of the hope that had accumulated within the past three weeks. More than that, I let go of the small kernel of hope that had flickered to life since I heard from Ghada two months ago. I took a final, steadying breath and let the flicker fade.

My dad squeezed us one more time before releasing us.

My mom held on as I wiped my tears. She said, "If you achieved absolutely nothing, we would still be proud of you. And it's because of who you grew up to be. You're smart, and kind, and brave. Now, not only are you all those things, but you're in a country far away, working hard to get your doctorate degree, and you're doing it all on your own."

"Had this project gone through, we would have been proud, but we don't need it to know that our daughter is great. You've shown us that all on your own," my dad added.

"We're proud of you too, if only for the fact that you had to put up with us," Hessa said, and I drank in their words like it was the first sip of water after a full day of fasting.

This is why I loved being home. To be surrounded by people who knew how to keep you sane was a privilege I missed.

"Go wash your face and come help with setting the table," my mom said gently.

I did as instructed and worked together to ready the table. Sara, Hessa, and I formed a chain from the kitchen to the dining table and passed cutlery and food between us just in time to break our fast. We sat around the table and talked about unimportant things.

For the rest of the night, we stayed up watching TV, eating leftover food, and playing cards. It was simple, but it was perfect in its simplicity. Everyone went to bed since Wednesday and the middle of the work week, but I stayed up. I opened my dissertation on my computer and reminded myself I still had something going for me. I wrote all night long, prayed fajr, and continued until the sun rose. When I couldn't keep my eyes open any longer, I went to sleep.

Twenty-One

I woke up groggy the next morning. At least, I assumed it was morning until I checked the time on my phone. The big numbers telling me it was two-thirty was less of a shock than the forty message notifications, and sixteen missed calls I had from Khalid. Panic was building inside me, and I hastily got up to open the thread of messages on my home screen first. They were all just different versions of my name and exclamation points. He didn't know I kept my phone on silent while I slept.

Too worked up to read through the rest of the messages, I called Khalid. He answered before it even got a chance to finish the first ring.

"Noor! Where have you been? I've been trying to reach you since this morning." I was going to explain that I was asleep, but he continued abruptly, "Never mind, that's not important. You need to come to DIFC right now. It's important. I got news this morning, and he wants to see you right now. Today. How soon can you meet me in the parking lot?"

He sounded so frantic that I didn't ask any questions. I told him I could meet him in half an hour and hung up the phone. I didn't know what was happening, but if Khalid said it was important, then it must be.

I got dressed in record time, throwing on a variation of yesterday's clothes, and ran down the stairs and out the door. I got onto the highway and found myself in the middle of rush hour. It wasn't bumper to bumper, but there were enough cars that it took me longer than usual to reach DIFC. On the bright side, the parking lot was virtually empty. I saw Khalid's car near the entrance and a free spot next to him. Khalid was out of his car and by my door before I'd even changed the gear to park. He opened the door as I grabbed my bag.

"Finally," he said by way of greeting.

"What's going on?" He shut the door behind me and pivoted towards the business buildings. I had to hop-skip to keep up with him. "Is it another investor?" My heart picked up speed, wondering if maybe there was still a small chance.

Khalid grinned and said, "No."

I didn't get why he was smiling. That didn't sound like a good thing.

He continued. "It's not a new investor. It's Ibrahim. He called me early this morning and said he had to speak with you. He was restless on the phone. Honestly, he sounded pretty upset."

"That doesn't sound good. Why do you seem excited about this?" I asked. We were already across the road and heading to what I now understood was Mr. Ibrahim's building.

"Because, Noor, he didn't say exactly what he wanted, but wanting to speak with you again is a good thing. Even if he was upset. It means he's reevaluating his decision. He might not change his mind, even after speaking with you now, but it means you have another chance to convince him."

I rubbed my forehead against the migraine I could feel forming. The back and forth with these investors was giving me whiplash. I couldn't keep up. This was all happening too fast on too little sleep. I can't have any coffee, and now my brain was punishing me for making it work extra hard to keep up with the unfolding events.

"Okay, so I'll talk to him again, but I'm not raising my hopes. You said he might still say no."

We reached the bottom of Mr. Ibrahim's building and stepped into the elevator, Khalid pushing the button for his floor.

I took a second to catch my breath. The fast walk did a number on me. Khalid didn't look winded at all. It was like an electric wire was plugged into him, and he was so full of vigor.

"Can you stop?"

"Stop what?" he asked.

"Stop that energy. It's too early." I glared at him. "My brain is still sleeping and doesn't appreciate your excited energy."

"This *is* exciting. I know something good is going to come out of this."

"I'm still not raising my hopes up."

He just grinned.

The elevator dinged, and we stepped off onto Mr. Ibrahim's floor. We were back full circle. Maybe it was the familiarity with the area or the small sense of belonging I feel now that I've walked these roads and know these people, but I felt calm. I glanced at Khalid. Maybe it was the familiarity with him.

We started toward the reception but came to a stop when we saw Mr. Ibrahim standing in the foyer. He wasn't standing exactly; he was pacing. His nervous energy, mixed with Khalid's excited energy, had my heart pounding. It felt like I was a lightning pole, directing their energies straight into me. I needed a nap.

Mr. Ibrahim spotted us and marched towards us.

"Hello, Mr. Ibrahim," I said. He shook his head.

"Call me Ibrahim. I'm so glad you could make it,

Noor. Khalid, thank you for arranging this," Ibrahim said. "Follow me." He turned around and marched into his office.

Khalid and I shared a look before we started after him. Once in his office, we sat on the chairs in front of his desk, but instead of sitting on the other side, Ibrahim pulled his chair around the desk and placed it between Khalid and I. Khalid and I shared another look before we shifted our chairs so that we were facing him.

Ibrahim settled himself and shifted in his chair so that he was almost directly facing me. "Noor, I'd like to start off by apologizing to you. Something has brought to my attention the fact that I did not really listen to you when you were giving me your pitch. I'm an old man, but I like to think I'm current. I've always sought ideas and projects that take society one step forward. You came to me with such an idea, and I was too confounded by the newness of it that I didn't quite see its full potential."

What he was saying was kind, but it didn't explain why he was in such a hurry to speak with me or his franticness. There was a hint of more behind his words, but honestly, he could have just sent me an email. Khalid didn't say anything. I would say he was holding his breath if I didn't know any better.

"Mr. Ibrahim—" I stopped abruptly and

corrupted myself when he pierced me with a look. "Ibrahim," I corrected, and he smiled approvingly. "I appreciate you telling me this. After the week I've had, it's honestly a consolation knowing you believe in the idea. But, may I ask, why the sudden change and why the rush?" I would dissolve into a puddle of exasperation if he didn't tell me.

"I'll tell you why. I spoke with Alaa." Khalid and I both cringed at the name, and Ibrahim noticed. "Yes, I'm aware of what happened during your meeting with her. I happened to be at an investor iftar yesterday that she was also attending. I sat across from her as she went on and on about a project she was pitched. I knew straight away she was talking about your idea—no one has approached us with an idea this novel and ambitious in a while. I couldn't believe what she was saying. It is one thing to disagree and entirely another to publicly criticize. Especially when there is nothing fundamentally wrong with the idea."

Heat flooded my face as I pictured a highly respected member of the investor community trashing my idea in front of others.

Ibrahim continued. "I couldn't sit there and tolerate it. I let her know exactly what I thought of her behavior. I was so ruffled that I moved tables. However, once I was seated with a plate of food in front of me, I couldn't eat. Her words didn't sit well with me. We both turned down your pitch. I couldn't imagine being on the same side as a person who acted like that. That's when I realized it. I didn't approve of Alaa's behavior because I disagreed with her wholeheartedly. Your idea was fantastic. Is fantastic. It should be subsidized. I phoned Khalid this morning to find out what happened. When he told me about this past week and your deadline on Friday, I knew this was my chance."

I sat up straighter in my chair, not quite believing what I was hearing. Khalid leaned forward in his own chair. My mouth was dry, and my head was pounding, and my heart matched its rhythm.

Ibrahim gave me a conspiratorial grin before he said, "I want to back you. I will invest in this research facility. And I would be delighted if you accepted."

It was a little difficult to hear him over the blood rushing in my ears, but I still heard his words. And in the time it took for the vibrations to travel through my ear canal and translate into electrical impulses that made their way to my brain, I grinned as wide as the Cheshire Cat.

After all the ups and downs of the past week, I was ecstatic to finally have this moment. It would have been so easy to give up after the first 'no,' or the second, or the third. It would have been simple to convince myself that I did enough by just emailing out my proposal. But had I stopped at those points, I never would have reached this one. It's very easy to assume that the middle of a journey is the end of it. That is until you take the next step.

Ibrahim and Khalid matched my grin, and he thumped Ibrahim in the back good-naturedly.

"What do you say, Noor?" Ibrahim asked.

What else was there to say?

"I say yes."

At that moment, I was thankful. I was thankful for my own annoying persistence, for Khalid's presence, for my friends who came up with a ridiculous scheme to buy me time, for my family whose advice gave me a solution to my problem, and for everyone's support and faith that carried me forward.

"I'll leave and let you guys talk," Khalid said and stood.

"No, you're not." The look I gave him was hard enough to crumble stone. "Sit down." He did.

With that settled, we spent the next hour in Ibrahim's office talking logistics. He wanted to know more about the financial aspect of the business. I told him everything I could. I assured him I would get an official agreement to rent out lab space from the companies I spoke to. He told me the sum his company would invest, and I nearly fainted at the number. It was enough, more than enough.

I also had to tell Ibrahim that I would be out of

the country for the next six months while I completed my PhD. He completely understood and assured me that it was not a problem. The beginning phase of the project would be about getting the details fleshed out. Email and video calls would suffice. I was relieved at the thought of not having to fly back and forth between my PhD studies and my new CEO duties. I was giddy at the thought. I was a CEO. I was getting my own research facility. It was happening.

Khalid and I said goodbye to Ibrahim. Before we left, I invited him to the meeting with Ghada on Friday so they could go over the fine points of the deal. In truth, I didn't want to tell Ghada about the troubles of the past week without my new investor there to assure her everything would continue as planned.

As we stepped out of Ibrahim's office, I inhaled the entire universe and exhaled all the stress and nerves and heartache that came from this exhausting but rewarding experience. Khalid heard it and chuckled, which got me giggling, which prompted him to laugh, which had us both gasping for air. I leaned against the wall to prevent myself from collapsing on the floor. Ibrahim stepped out of his office and peered down the hall at us. He just shook his head and walked back in. The giggles subsided, and I motioned Khalid to the elevators before we made bigger fools of ourselves. When the elevator doors closed behind us, I turned to Khalid.

"I can't believe it. Please pinch me. I was so sure yesterday was the end of it, and now, I have a research facility in development. Why aren't you pinching me?" I could hear the hysteria in my voice. It would take me a week, maybe a month, to recover after all this.

"I'm not pinching you because you're not dreaming. You did it." He beamed as he said it.

I repeated those three words over and over in my head, but I must have been whispering them to myself because Khalid looked over as we exited the building, looking thoroughly amused. I didn't mind it. I wanted to do more than whisper it to myself. I wanted to climb Mt. Everest and scream it to the entire world. Since I was physically incapable of doing that, I did the next best thing and yelled it aloud once we reached the empty parking lot.

"Did you purposely wait until there was no one around?" Khalid asked, chuckling and rubbing his head.

"I did. There's no reason to subject others to my mania."

"What about me? Do I not count?"

If I had to make a list of people who mattered the most, Khalid would be right on top. I looked at him now as he squinted in the midday sun, smiling at me like I was the source of all his happiness, the world grew still for the smallest, most significant moment.

This person. I wanted to keep this person around.

Instead of telling him all the things I wanted to say, I said, "Nope, you're in this a hundred percent, my friend. There's no backing out now. Besides, you have to stick around to translate all the fancy finance terms for me. I can't look up everything."

"Why do I have the feeling I'm going to be getting a lot of random articles to translate for you at one in the morning?"

"Because of the time zone difference, silly. And just articles? I was thinking more along the lines of entire documents. Big bulky documents." I was making awkward gestures with my hand, attempting to mime bulky documents to him. *Why am I so embarrassing?* I stopped with the hand gestures and said, "We can sort out the technicalities later."

We were at our cars at this point, with not much left to say except goodbye. Khalid seemed to sense it, too, but still, we stayed. Not quite ready to leave.

"I'm so glad we'll be giving Ghada good news," I said.

"I'm so glad you have good news to give," Khalid answered, gently tapping my shoe with his. The movement brought him closer.

I managed to speak again after breathing past a heart palpation. "Me, too. Have I said thank you? Even if I have, thank you so much. None of this would have been possible without you."

"It's been my pleasure, Noor."

I most definitely did not stare at his mouth. Time to go. I inched towards my car. "I guess I'll see you on Friday then."

"Friday." He said it like a promise and disappeared into his car.

Twenty~Two

It was officially my last week in Dubai. It would be full of bittersweet moments; for every gathering I could attend, I'd remember I would miss out on so many more for the next six months.

I spent all day Friday at the mall with Hessa, Sara, Mona, and Hana. We spent hours going from store to store, trying on clothes and shoes. We spent so long in one of the changing rooms that the store clerks came in and asked us if we were okay. We all ended up with outfits that we were excited to show off.

I spent Saturday doing virtually nothing. It was the first time in a long time that I lazed around the house, aimlessly watching TV. I did a group call with Lamya, Maha, Aysha, and Heba to inform them that we needed to celebrate. We decided to gather that night.

This week was also the last five days of Ramadan, which meant that a lot of our nights were spent praying and reading more Qur'an to commemorate the day Islam began. Eid al Fitr was soon, too.

After fasting for nearly thirty days, the first thing I wanted to do on Eid morning was go out for breakfast and order a huge cup of coffee. Then I would come home, get dressed in my new clothes, and head over to my uncle's house, where everyone in the family would also be to celebrate. It was such a joyous occasion. I couldn't wait.

Finally, Friday. I would walk up to Ghada with my head held high and let her know that I had an investor backing the project and that we could begin development. Fifteen-year-old me would be so proud. It looked like my ten-year plan was about to start.

I was excited to get the project underway, so excited that I reached Ghada's office a whole forty-five minutes earlier than scheduled. I let reception know who I was going to see and took a seat in the waiting area. I was idly scrolling through social media when Ghada passed by with a tablet in her hand, wearing a beautiful navy-blue abaya with lapels in the front, mimicking a blazer, looking every inch the CEO of a business incubator.

"Noor! You're early," she said.

"I know," I said, a little embarrassed. "Don't

mind me. I'll just wait until it's closer to the meeting time."

"Don't be silly. Come to my office. I don't have much to do other than wait for the meeting to start, too. We can wait together." She smiled encouragingly at me, and I was immediately grateful. Not only were these people helping me accomplish something I always thought would just be a dream, but they were also incredibly amiable.

Ghada and I walked to her office together, chatting about our plans for Eid on the way.

"You really have seventy-five people over for Eid?" I asked. She chuckled as she opened the door for me.

"And that's only on my father's side of the family. Please, sit."

I settled in my seat, and we continued talking. I asked her about her background and how she came to start a business incubator. I was curious to know her journey and see if it resembled mine in any way. Ghada said that she had followed the typical route of graduating from university before starting out in the corporate world, but even though she was progressing in her career, she felt that there was more she wanted to do outside the confines of a nine-to-five. So, she quit her job and started a small home business selling her paintings online—she pointed out the various art hanging around her office that turned out to be hers.

Despite her parents' frustration at her choices, she continued with her craft until she wanted more and decided to open her own gallery. She initially found the process overwhelming. She didn't know where to start or who to turn to. After persevering and opening a gallery, she decided she wanted to make the process of starting a business easier for others. That's why she started HighRise.

What I learned was this: everyone's journey is their own. There's no single formula that guarantees success. Sometimes, you just have to go where your path takes you. And if you're struggling, you have to be willing to share your limitations with others. No one will know you need help until you show them that you're struggling.

I recalled how I needed help but didn't ask anyone because I was too scared of failing. Had I not said anything, my friends wouldn't have been able to buy me time, and my uncle wouldn't have guided me to a revenue solution. There was no shame in asking for help.

After what felt like no time at all, reception phoned Ghada to let her know that Khalid and Ibrahim were on their way in. I wasn't going to lie; I was a little bummed at being interrupted. Ghada was pretty cool. Khalid and Ibrahim stepped into the office a moment later.

My gaze fell on Khalid just as he locked on mine, my smile already in place, and his tugged from a small smile to a full grin. He huffed a laugh to himself and shook his head, turning towards Ibrahim and Ghada.

Ghada greeted them. I had sent her an email telling her that Ibrahim would be joining us for the meeting and that I would explain why today. She went with it and graciously agreed, no questions asked. She already knew Khalid, so he introduced Ibrahim to her. They made small talk for a while until the pleasantries slowly slipped away, making room for the crux of the matter. Ghada gestured for us to sit around the small coffee table.

Ghada turned to me. "Tell me you have good news for me." I shook my head in a way to tell her, *you have no idea*. She said, "Tell me everything."

"So," I started. "After our initial meeting, Khalid and I got together to discuss the best way to proceed as partners on the project. It took a few weeks." I gave Khalid an amused, knowing look. He returned it. "But we eventually reached a conclusion that met both our needs with regard to the institute. However, a week ago, Khalid's company had money troubles, and sadly, it went under. That left me without an investor backing the project. Khalid was gracious enough to help me find a different source for funding."

"That explains Ibrahim, then," Ghada said.

"Yes. We spent all of last week meeting with potential investors, and Ibrahim was one of them.

We've discussed the plans for the project, and he's agreed to fund me. So, although it took a few turns, the project has an investor." I declared it proudly. The sheer amount of work it took to finally be able to say that sentence deserved to be recognized.

Ghada looked stunned. She turned to Khalid first. "Khalid! I never heard the news about your company. As one of our leading investors, I thought I would hear of such news."

"I'm sure you will be notified soon. It happened last week, and the last thing I heard was that they wanted to do some damage control to save whatever is left of their reputation. I would have told you myself, but I wanted to make sure Noor could guarantee you alternate funding first." He looked sincerely apologetic, and I was abashed at not mentioning any of this to Ghada earlier. I was scared that she'd pull the plug on the whole project.

She turned to Ibrahim next. "Ibrahim, thank you so much for stepping in. I'm sure you see how essential Noor's project is since you've agreed to fund it."

"I do. It may have taken a bit of convincing, truth be told, but the realization hit me like a bolt of lightning. A scientific research institute that offers hands-on learning for students and gradu- ates. It'll open many new doorways."

"I agree. I look forward to working with you on this."

"As am I."

Finally, she turned to me and smiled. "Well, it seems like you've had an interesting few weeks."

"It's been quite the rollercoaster."

"One of the things we help with here at the incubator is locating a source of funding. It's supposed to ease the way for you. The fact that you've had to find one on your own tells me a lot about your character. It's unfortunate you struggled with it, but it shows me how passionate and determined you are to turn your idea into concrete and metal. I admire your drive."

I was filled with warm and fuzzy feelings hearing her say it. "Thank you. I can't tell you how much that means to me." She dipped her head in acknowledgment.

"Since I have you all here, I think it's time we make everything official and sign some contracts." She opened a drawer in her desk and pulled out four stacks of documents. She handed me two and scribbled something on the other two before passing them to Ibrahim. "Noor, this is your contract and a copy. Please feel free to look through it before you sign. Ibrahim, this is yours, declaring you as the investor and the features you'll be covering, so if you could just sign the end.

We took a moment to scan through the documents. Everything seemed to be in order. I signed and initialed my set of documents. We handed all the documents back to Ghada, and she placed her signature on them and then handed us back our copies. Ibrahim pulled out his stack of papers and handed them to Ghada and me. These were contracts from the company he worked at, stating the funding fees, as well as other technicalities. He and Ghada went back and forth about it, and Khalid contributed to the discussion before they came to an agreement, and we all signed those documents.

I wondered how Khalid was feeling. I couldn't stop the little pang of disappointment at the thought that we wouldn't be working together. The past weeks had shown how great we were at working together. It was easy and exciting, and we did a great job propping each other up. Working together felt like we could take on a hundred more Alaas if we wanted to. Which I definitely did not want to, but it's the thought that counts.

Khalid caught me staring, and for a brief moment, his regular professional poker face was wiped away and replaced with excitement. I wanted to smack him—good-naturedly, but still. Instead of feeling sorry for himself over losing this opportunity, he was just happy for me. The man had no self-preservation. He must have seen the thoughts written on my face—since my poker face was nowhere near as good as his—because his features rearranged themselves to bewilderment. I shook my head at him and handed the documents back to Ibrahim. I needed to ask Khalid about his job interviews later.

Ghada clapped her hands together. "Well, I would normally invite you all out for lunch to celebrate this union, but that'll have to wait until after Ramadan. Ibrahim, thank you so much for coming today and for your support. Noor, thank you for providing us with this opportunity."

"Thank *you* for this opportunity. I still can't believe it's happening," I replied.

"I'm sure it'll hit you once we get your business card printed out. CEO in bold letters usually does the trick." She smiled, and I couldn't have stopped the smile I returned had I tried.

The meeting wasn't over yet. We spent the next hour discussing timelines, micro-projects, potential locations, and staff hiring. We couldn't go through everything in an hour, but we went through enough to get a general outline of what would happen in the next couple of years. I was grateful I was almost done with my PhD because the next couple of years looked like it would keep me *busy*.

Twenty~Three

The meeting wrapped up, and we all said our goodbyes. I couldn't give Khalid the bashing he deserved because Ibrahim left with us. We had also parked in different locations, so we said our goodbyes and parted ways.

While stopped at a traffic light, I opened a text.

> May I ask why you looked upset for a duration of time during the meeting? I was very well-behaved.

I read the message and put my phone away as the light turned green. I waited until I was back home before I responded. When I checked my phone again, Khalid had sent more messages.

My first interview is tomorrow, by
the way. And I have another one the
day after.

Now that I had what I wanted, I truly wanted
him to get the job he wanted as well. I wished I had
made friends with some business-type people so
that I could've helped him out. Maybe if he landed
one of the jobs—which I was sure he would—we
could celebrate before I left this upcoming
Saturday.

Sorry for taking so long to respond.
I was driving.

Tell me how the interviews go
afterward.

When is the financial consultant
one? That's the one you wanted
right?

How did you feel during the
meeting?

I was prying for information. I wanted to know
if he was upset at all. He's good at hiding his
emotions, but I know him better now.

Is this a trick question? I was happy.
Ecstatic really. The past week has
been one twisted roller coaster ride.
I'm so glad we finally found you an
investor.

You weren't disappointed?

Even a little bit?

Not at all. Why would I be? I've wanted to see this project go through ever since Ghada sent me your proposal. There is nothing disappointing about today. Are you disappointed? Do you not like Ibrahim?

No, no. Ibrahim is great.

I just wish it was you and I, like it has been the last three weeks.

Why wouldn't it be? You're not getting rid of me that easily. I now take my job as your financial connoisseur very seriously.

I get the feeling that I'm going to regret asking for your help.

Only sometimes.

Fantastic.

Hessa and Sara walked through the door just then and caught me smiling at my phone.

"What's so funny?" Hessa asked.

"Hi to you, too."

"Oh! Noor! How was your meeting?" Sara dumped her things on the couch and sat by me. Hessa followed her lead and sat on my other side.

They looked at me expectantly, their eyes

shining in excitement. For a split second, I considered pranking them, pretending it didn't work out...

"I see you scheming! Stop that, and just tell us!" Hessa exclaimed. I threw my arms around their shoulders.

"You are now blessed by the presence of the CEO of the upcoming learning-based research facility in Dubai."

Their joint screams pierced my ears, and I squeezed them tight. We made fun of each other, got mad at each other, and scapegoated each other to avoid trouble with the parents, but I couldn't imagine a world without them.

My parents arrived home later on, and I shared the good news with them. And just like at the beginning of Ramadan, the news spread through the family grapevine like wildfire. My uncle invited the whole family over for iftar that night. By the time I reached, everyone was well aware, and 'congratulations' was thrown around like confetti. Mona and Hana even made me a cake.

We broke our fasts and sat together in the living room. I huddled between Hessa and Hana, Sara and Mona on their other sides. Their body heat seeped through me, and I relaxed. At first, everyone asked me about the progress of the research institute. I told them what would be happening within the next year.

"Who would have thought a degree in chemistry would lead to you opening your own lab? Guess it wasn't useless after all." This came from Mohammed.

Before I had the chance to reply—or smack him—Ahmed leaned over and shoved his shoulder.

"It was never useless. You just couldn't understand its importance," he said. He looked over at me and winked. I smiled gratefully. "Besides, it's a degree in drug design and manufacturing." He beamed at me proudly and continued eating his cake slice. Bless him; he really did try.

Hana leaned over Hessa and asked, clearly confused, "It's genetics and molecular biology though, right?"

"Yes. At least someone knows what it is."

"Oh, don't get me wrong. I have the name memorized, but I have no idea what it actually means. And please don't explain again. It makes my head hurt," she said.

I leaned forward and cut myself a second piece of cake. As I settled back to dig in, I picked up on my dad's conversation with my uncle across from us.

"...it wasn't until I did a diagnostic test that I found out he suggested bad suppliers. I had to fire him. I'm interviewing for a new financial consultant on Tuesday. One of the candidates, Khalid, has very high potential. His track record is very impressive. The others are great too, but…"

He couldn't mean my Khalid, could he? This could be my moment to help him—I could put in a good word for him with my uncle.

I cleared my throat. "'Amo Ahmed," I called. He stopped talking and looked over at me, along with my father. "I overheard you speaking and realized I knew one of the candidates, Khalid." My uncle and dad shared a glance before looking back.

"How do you know Khalid?" my uncle asked.

"His company was supposed to invest in my project. I met with Khalid before his company went bankrupt. After he lost his job and I the investment, he helped me find my new investor."

"What can you tell me about his work ethic?"

"He's very determined, has never been late for a meeting, handles stressful situations with a practiced hand, and is level-headed." Recounting his qualities was as easy as counting to ten.

"He didn't walk away when you were left fundless either, which tells me he takes accountability for his actions. Or, in this case, his company's actions," Amo Ahmed added. "Very well. I'll, of course, confirm with his list of references, but he seems fit for the job. His qualifications alone would have given him the position. Thank you, Noor."

"You're welcome." I returned to my cake, acting cool, but I was so excited.

While my uncle wouldn't hire Khalid just because I said so, the fact that he saw Khalid's merit on his own made me so proud. Khalid worked so hard to reach the point where people believed in his capabilities.

Finally reassured that Khalid was taken care of, I relaxed on the couch and took a bite. The vanilla icing never tasted so good.

CHAPTER
Twenty~Four

I spent two hours with my family before going to Maha's. It was only ten minutes before I pulled up to the house and noticed I was the first to arrive. I parked the car and walked straight into the house. Her husband was out, so we had the house to ourselves.

"Maha!" I shouted once I closed the door behind me.

"I'm over here!" she shouted back. "And don't yell! The baby is sleeping!"

I followed the sound of her voice and found her in the living room on the ground floor of her two-story house. Maha's house style was as clean and elegant as she was, with neutral color schemes in shades of beige and white tied in with light-brown wood accents. The outside of the house was more modern, matching the other houses in the residential complex with its white façade and endless windows.

"Did you realize how ironic you were being when you yelled at me to keep quiet?" I said by way of greeting. Maha was sitting on the couch, playing on her phone. Baby Jasim was nowhere to be seen.

"I'm allowed to wake him up. No one else is. Mother privileges."

"How about you wake him up now and bring him so I can play with him?" I walked over to her and gave her a hug. "You know I only have a finite amount of time left to squeeze his cheeks."

"You'll only be gone for six months this time. You'll be back in no time at all."

"But six months of no Jasim is the equivalent of six months with no Arabic coffee. You can survive, but your life is all the bleaker without it."

"But you take Arabic coffee with you."

"Exactly, so I have to soak up my time with Jasim to take the memories with me." Just as I said this, Maha's baby monitor sounded with Jasim's cries. I looked at Maha in triumph. She chuckled and left the room, returning with our little bundle of joy, and handed him to me.

Jasim and I had a wonderful conversation consisting of squeaky baby talk from me and strange looks from him.

Maha sat beside me. "Where's everyone else?" I asked.

"Lamya said she'd be half an hour late, and Aysha should be here soon."

"That's strange. Lamya is usually the first one here. Did she say what was holding her up?" I asked.

"She did not, but I'm sure she'll tell us once she's here." She leaned down and kissed Jasim's forehead.

I smiled fondly at the sight. We always knew Maha would be a great mom. Jasim was a blessed kid. Maha offered me a bottle of milk, and I accepted the opportunity to feed him.

We heard the front door open, followed by a loud "Hello!"

Aysha arrived.

"We're in the living room," I answered.

Aysha barreled into the room. "I have arrived. Ooooh, potato!" She spotted Jasim and came straight for him. She gently lifted him from my arms and took over, feeding him the rest of his bottle.

"Where's Lamya?" she asked.

"She'll be here in half an hour," Maha told her.

"But I'm hungry now," she complained. Maha's glare was enough of a scold that Aysha conceded.

"How's your new collection coming along?" I asked Aysha, remembering the art gallery she mentioned at the hospital.

"It's fantastic if I do say so myself. It's a poetic

demonstration of the urban development in our little piece of the world."

"Are you just going to take pictures of the Bastakiya area, then pictures of Sheikh Zayed Road's skyscrapers?" Maha asked.

"Yes, but I'm going to use a drone to take pictures of the different structures from the top looking down. That way, when you get to the Burj Khalifa picture, you'll feel the elevation. Each step through the gallery will make you feel like you're rising, too."

"Please tell me it won't be ready until I return. I have to see this," I said.

"It'll be ready exactly when it's ready. But I'll hold off on the gallery display until you're back."

I put an arm around her and hugged her tight, minding Jasim. "You're amazing, you know that?"

"Yes, I'm fully aware," she said.

Maha and I shared a smile because we knew it was true. One personality trait that stuck with Aysha through all the years I've known her is her confidence and utter belief in herself.

Aysha was timid when we first met back in the seventh grade. She had a bad time at her old school, where her classmates bullied her. She didn't tell us any of this when our friendship was growing, but we noticed a change in her that year. She finished the seventh grade as a boisterous, self-appreciating human being. We didn't question it at the time. We just enjoyed the ride.

It wasn't until some years later that she explained it to us. After being teased for years, she said she finally found a place where she could be herself. The first time she voiced her opinion, we hadn't mocked her. The first time she put on her glasses, we didn't insult her appearance. The first time she invited us over, we showed up. She said that that was when she realized she could be more open. We all cried when she told us the whole story. Now, ten years later, it was hard to imagine Aysha being timid.

Maha took Jasim once Aysha finished feeding him his bottle and burped him. We walked about motherhood and what makes a good picture great.

Exactly half an hour on the dot, we heard the front door open again. Before Lamya could ask, we all called out where we were, startling Jasim in the process. Maha soothed him, and we froze as we waited to see whether or not he would cry. He must have decided he wasn't scared because he didn't cry. We relaxed and turned to the door just as Lamya walked in. She smiled and looked over her shoulder at something. Maha, Aysha, and I shared confused looks.

We focused back on Lamya as she entered the room completely, and behind her walked Heba. You could hear a pin drop in the moment of stunned silence before we all jumped up and attacked her in a crushing group hug—well, all of us, minus Maha and Jasim.

There are moments when the joy you feel is so immense that it is impossible to keep bottled up, and so it bursts out in uncontrollable fits of laughter. That's how I felt as I hugged my best friends. You have to travel the globe in search of adventure to realize that the only place you want to travel to is home.

We extricated ourselves from the hug. Heba had tears running down her face that she brushed away as we made space for Maha to hug her.

The guest living room was large, with many couches lining the four walls. We ditched them all in favor of close proximity and huddled on the floor together, our knees touching each other's.

"When did you get here?" Maha asked Heba.

"Today. Just now. I had Lamya pick me up from the airport."

"Um, excuse me, why were we not informed?" This came from a slightly insulted Aysha.

"I wanted to surprise you, obviously." Heba rolled her eyes. I chuckled. "I made the decision a week after Noor arrived. Everything that was happening sounded so fun and exciting, and I hadn't celebrated Eid at home in forever. I had to wait until I got some work done, which is why I'm here so late, but at least I'm here." She took a deep breath and grinned. "So, where are we going to have breakfast on Eid morning?"

"That place by the beach," Aysha said.

"No, the restaurant we went to the last time Noor was here," Maha said.

"Are you sure you can even come with the baby?" Lamya asked.

"Of course, she can come with the baby. It's just a baby. It'll sleep while we eat," Aysha responded.

"Everyone's going, no exceptions," I said. "We haven't all had Eid breakfast together since forever, and we're all here now."

"So, we are going to the place by the beach?" Aysha hedged.

"No, let's go to Barari," Heba added.

"Barari is so far," Aysha moaned.

"But it's pretty!"

"It's far!"

"The baby!"

We all stilled and looked at Jasim. He was sitting quietly in Maha's arms, so I had no idea why she blurted it out. I looked at her questioningly.

"What's wrong with the baby?" I asked.

"Nothing's wrong with the baby. But as the mother of a newborn, I get dibs on restaurant choice."

Aysha groaned and slumped forward. "That's not fair. You made up that rule!"

"If you want to make up some rules, have your

own baby. Until then, we're going to Home Bakery."

I chuckled at Aysha's defeated expression.

"Where am I supposed to get a baby from anyways? I don't even have a love interest." Aysha said.

"Not my problem."

"It'll be Noor who has a baby next," Lamya said, wiggling her brows at me.

I could feel heat pooling in my cheeks.

"What? Why me?" My voice may have gone up an octave.

Lamya looked down, examining her nails. The perfect picture of nonchalance. "Oh, no reason. It's not like you've been spending an obscene amount of time with a certain finance expert."

"Is she talking about Khalid?" Heba whispered loudly to Maha. Maha looked at her and nodded her head, grinning. Aysha leaned forward, her elbows braced on her knees and cupping her face in her hands.

"It's just business!" I shot back. There were only so many times I could repeat myself, and this group right here was testing the limit.

"So, you're never going to speak to him again after today?" Lamya asked.

"Well, no, I am. But that's because he has to update me on his job interviews, and he's my unofficial finance translator." I took Jasim from Maha and snuggled him. She didn't deserve baby snuggles while she was interrogating me.

"Wait, why did you make him your translator? I'm sure you don't actually need someone to translate the words for you. That's what the internet is for," Heba said.

"Yes, but I think it'll be easier to just message Khalid."

"Why don't you just admit you did this so that you would still have a reason to talk to him?" Aysha insisted.

I glared at each of them in turn and then sighed in defeat.

"Okay, fine. Maybe I did. But it's just because we've become good friends."

"How can she be this in denial?" Heba whispered loudly again, but this time to Aysha.

"You know I can hear you, right? I'm sitting right here—on your other side."

"Noor, *hayati,* think about it for a moment. We are the perfect friends. You have no reason to need new ones. So, what is it about Khalid that made you want to keep him as a *friend*? Why do you like him?"

Heba said the word 'friend' so sarcastically that I narrowed my eyes at her, but I contemplated her question. Why did I like Khalid? There were so many reasons. He was sweet, kind, supportive, encouraging, determined, passionate—he showed an interest in what I loved, and he fought for my dreams even when his career took a plunge. I remembered how passive his expression was when I first met him and how engaged he was with me now. We really did become partners these past weeks.

Those were all my favorite things about him, and as I listed them in my head, the different moments we had together came into view: the soft smiles and sweet words, the playful attitude and easy-going nature. Moments I probably shouldn't have shared with a business associate, but I did because I was comfortable in his presence. Moments I definitely wouldn't have shared with just a friend. And as future moments of my life unfolded, I imagined Khalid being there—a steady presence in the face of life's turmoil and a companion for life's adventures. I tried to imagine someone else, another blurry-faced man, but I just couldn't. No one else would support me the way Khalid did.

I sighed deeply and collapsed on the floor, my head on Lamya's lap and my arms and legs spread across Aysha, Maha, and Heba.

"What am I supposed to do with this information now?" I asked.

"Tell Khalid?" This came from Aysha.

I glared at her. "I can't tell him. How would I tell? He probably doesn't even like me like that."

"Umm, I'm going to hedge a guess and say that he does," Heba said.

"You didn't even meet him."

"I don't need to meet him. Why would a VC spend so much of his time helping you if he didn't like you?"

"He likes my idea and wants to see it established. That's it." I got a little sad at the thought. *That couldn't be it, could it?*

"I think she's finally starting to get it," Maha said to the circle. I sat up and looked at the faces I had grown up with. The people I trusted the most.

Lamya looked at me fondly and said, "I'm thrilled you're going to find your love story. Tell him. You'll be glad you did."

It was Thursday morning, Eid morning. Thirty days of fasting was complete, and I was finally back to delicious, life-saving morning coffee. There's an excited buzz that comes with the first fast-free morning. You wake up feeling accomplished and invigorated. Eid is an occasion to celebrate your religious accomplishment. Everyone gets squeaky clean, dressed in new clothes, and heads out to celebrate with family and friends. And that's just what I did.

I woke up bright and early to shower, do my makeup, and put on my new outfit. I was so proud of it. I ran to the mall at the last minute and managed to pull something decent together: I found a creamy linen set and matched it with a white scarf. I heard voices being carried between one room and the other and opened my door to the lively chatter that was my family getting ready as well.

"Eidkum mubarak, everyone!" I said as soon as I opened the door.

"Eidish Mubarak," came the reply from my mom, dad, and sisters at once from their rooms.

We hugged each other, and there was a wonderful sense of giddy joy in the air.

"Hessa, do you have my eyeliner?" Sara asked from her room.

"No, I gave it to you yesterday," Hessa replied from her own room.

"No, you didn't. You put it in your bag."

"It's not in my—oh, I have it."

"Bring it!"

"I'm busy!"

"Girls! Help each other out, it's Eid," my dad called from his bedroom.

I smiled at the familiarity of it all and went to get the eyeliner from Hessa and carry it to Sara. She didn't even look at me as she thanked me and started applying the eyeliner. I left her to finish getting dressed and make my way downstairs.

The table was already set with food that my mom had probably made for us before she went to get dressed herself. The aroma was making my mouth water, but I had plans with the girls for breakfast. My parents came down the stairs as I was putting on my shoes.

"You look nice, Noor."

"Thanks, Baba. You look handsome yourself."

"Are you sure? Is my ghutra straight?" he started fixing his headscarf as he said it. I approached him and straightened out the square white material he wrapped around his head. The round black cord, agal, was tilted, so I straightened that out, too.

"There, now you're perfect."

"Of course I'm perfect. Where do you think you get it from?"

I beamed at the compliment and laughed at his confidence before giving him a hug.

"Mama, you're perfect every day and look even more beautiful today," I told my mom and moved to hug her, too.

"That's because *I'm* the reason you're perfect. Now, sit and have some breakfast." She pulled out a chair and sat. My dad followed suit.

"I can't, Mama. The girls and I are heading out for breakfast like we used to before Heba and I left. It might be our only chance for a while." I could already hear her response in my head before she said it out loud.

"Why would you go out for breakfast on Eid morning when you can have perfectly good food at home? I thought you enjoyed my shakshouka." She was referring to the sunny-side-up egg currently bathing in deliciously spiced tomato sauce.

"I love your shakshouka, but we've had this tradition since we all turned eighteen, and I only have a few more days to see them. I'll see you at Amo Ahmed's for lunch." I took a piece of bread, scooped some of the egg and tomato sauce—one bite wouldn't kill my appetite—and rushed out the door.

Before I pulled out of the house, I sent a quick text to Khalid, wishing him a blessed Eid. We had been texting back and forth all week. He messaged me back on Monday, saying that his interview went well, but he didn't get the right vibes from his potential employer. I didn't mention my conversation with my uncle and told him hopefully, the next employer—my uncle—would have better energy.

His message Tuesday morning after the interview was the longest block message I have received from him thus far. He talked about what he thought of the employer, the company, the position, the office, the people he met, the office view, and the benefits. He talked about it *a lot* more than he talked about in his first interview. Clearly, he was excited. My uncle hadn't given him a response straight away, but I was sure he would any day now.

Messaging Khalid felt normal now. I didn't worry about sounding silly or wondering if he cared to hear what I had to say because I knew he did. The extent of how much he cared, I had yet to determine. He was always friendly, so it was hard to tell. But I would tell him soon. Sometimes, you just have to put your big girl pants on.

I arrived at Dubai Design District right on time. I parked the car and walked to Home Bakery, where Maha and Heba were already seated inside.

"What? Where's Jasim?! Maha!" I leaned down to give them hugs and sat, giving Maha my saddest, hurt puppy dog expression.

"Oh, relax. He was fussing, so Lamya took him for a walk."

I visibly relaxed. "Okay, good. Tell her to come back now." I nudged her phone, which was lying on the table, towards her. She rolled her eyes but picked up the phone.

"How long did you guys have to wait for a table?" I asked Heba.

"They told us it was a forty-minute wait, but I think someone canceled since they called us back after twenty minutes. This is why we have the arrive-extra-early-to-avoid-seating-problems contingency plan."

"Your plan is as brilliant as you are," I told Heba. "By the way, you both look picture-perfect. We need to take selfies before we leave."

It was true. Heba was dressed in a flowy white skirt with a white blouse tucked into it. The ensemble had her tan skin glowing—or it could have been the highlight she had on. Maha was wearing a baby pink abaya with gold patterns and cinched at the waist with a matching belt. All our clothes were made from light, flowy material to counter the hot summer day.

"You don't look too bad yourself, meeting anyone special today?" Maha asked.

"Who is more special to me than my wonderful, smart, and exceedingly annoying friends?" I smiled as I said it.

Lamya came in just then with Aysha and Jasim in his stroller.

"Look who I found," Lamya said as she placed Jasim near Maha and came to give me a hug. Aysha passed around the table for hugs, too. Hugs are such a wonderfully simple way to tell someone you care.

"Eidkum mubarak, my lovelies," Aysha said, taking a seat.

"Eidish mubarak, beautiful," Heba replied for us.

Aysha was far too busy studying the menu to acknowledge us any further. I opened up my own menu and flipped straight to the coffee section. I was feeling particularly fancy today and decided to order the long black. Just because I was feeling fancy didn't mean I had to subject my tastebuds to anything but the purest flavor of coffee.

The waiter came and took our drink orders. I

lifted Jasim out of his stroller and held him in my arms. Maha handed me a bottle, and I fed him.

"Now," Aysha started, "what are we having for breakfast? I propose we all order something different and share so that we all get a taste of everything. Good? Good."

"Nothing with tomato sauce. I don't want to spill anything on my clothes," Heba said.

I looked her dead in the eyes and said, "We have been friends for thirteen years. Don't let this ruin it. It will ruin it. I demand shakshouka!"

"I'm wearing white!"

"Borrow Jasim's bib!"

Neither of us could keep a straight face after that and burst out laughing. I, of course, ended up ordering the shakshouka and kept it as far away from Heba as possible, occasionally threatening to flick some sauce at her. It was good to have her back.

I glanced around the table as we dug into our food—and each other's. Including today, I had just two days left in Dubai. This outing was the last one I had with my girls. Tomorrow was reserved for my parents and sisters, and my flight was scheduled to leave early the next morning.

Just like that, my month was ending. I spent the last three days juggling between friends and family, like I had been doing all month, trying to get as many moments as possible with everyone. It was busy and hectic, but worth every hug and smile.

It would be another six months before I saw anyone again, but these moments would carry me through. It was only six months, after all. With tidying my research paper and sitting for the viva test, where I would have to defend my dissertation, time would pass in a blink. I would also deal with decisions that have to be made for the research institute. It would be a lot, but I was looking forward to it all. Great beginnings and all that.

There was just one loose end left.

"Please tell me how I should start the conversation with Khalid." I didn't need to explain more.

"You look him in the eye and tell him you'd like to see where this is going to go. Nice and simple," Maha said. Everything was nice and simple for Maha. Her water broke, and she was the picture of peace and serenity.

"Okay. I'll do that. What if it goes wrong? There's a huge possibility that this will go very wrong. Tell me what to do if this goes wrong." I was getting nervous just thinking about it. My heart was in my stomach, and electrical impulses were firing off every nerve ending in my body.

"First, breathe." Heba paused and looked at me expectantly. I stared back. "Now, Noor. Breathe now."

"Oh, okay. Okay. I'm breathing." I took in a deep breath and exhaled.

"Good," she said. "First of all, if he turns you down, then he's a moron who doesn't know what's good for him. Second of all, you are absolutely and positively one of the best people I know. What he chooses holds no bearing on you as a person. You are imperfectly perfect. Actually, make that first of all. Second of all, how stupid of a man he is if he turns down that kind of perfection."

"But I am perfectly perfect," I stated.

"*Ya Allah*. Noor! That's not the point," Lamya exclaimed.

"Of course, it's the point," Aysha backed me up. "Everything that she is and can be is her own definition of perfect. She is perfect because she is herself. Faults, and strengths, and weaknesses. That's the point."

"That's what I said," Heba retaliated.

"We're going off on a tangent," Maha said.

"Yes, let's regroup. Things won't go bad, so you don't need to worry about it," Lamya said. She saw me preparing to say something and stopped me. "That's it. End of discussion. Pass me your eggs."

I did as I was told.

We finished up breakfast and walked to the parking lot together. When we reached the point where we would have to go our separate ways, we huddled in a circle and spent half an hour saying our goodbyes.

"No one warned me that being an adult would include so many goodbyes," Lamya said, teary-eyed.

"Aww honey, it won't be for long this time." I hugged her tight one more time before letting go.

Heba sighs. "I hate that I only got less than a week with you."

"I'll be here permanently next time, and we'll have all the time in the world." Heba would be staying an additional two weeks before leaving to complete her studies.

I hugged each of them in turn and walked away before I spent another half hour saying more good-byes. It never got any easier, but that only meant that I was blessed, and for that, I was thankful.

I reached my uncle's house just as everyone else was arriving. I caught up with Mona and Hana and walked in with them. My family was already there, kissing everyone's cheeks three times. We formed a sort of line of new-to-arrived individuals making their way around the living room, saying hello to the already-arrived individuals.

Once everyone arrived and greeted each other, we sat down and ate lunch. I was still so full from breakfast, but that wasn't going to stop me from eating an entire plate of food.

My uncle signaled me from across the room just as I finished my plate and leaned back to breathe in

in one of the tables at the back. I slipped into the chair across from him. The staff offered us a complimentary cup of gahwa and dates in honor of Eid. I held the cup with both hands, breathing in the aroma and making a mental note to take enough coffee back with me.

"What are we getting to celebrate your achievement?" I asked without preamble, picking up the menu.

"We're getting the most chocolatey cake to celebrate our achievements. You also owe me a coffee."

I smiled in delight. "That's right. I do. Because I'm a CEO now. And you owe me coffee, too. Because you got a job. Wow, this is great." I leaned back in my chair, feeling pleased. It felt great to be able to say that with none of the stress and anxiety of the previous month.

The waiter took our order and came back with our steaming cups of coffee and slices of cake. Khalid practically ate half of it in one bite while I swallowed half of my coffee in one gulp.

"When do you start your new position?" I asked Khalid.

"Bright and early Monday morning. Salim, that's my boss, is putting me straight to work, analyzing the different projects the company is undertaking. I can't wait to start."

"Speaking of Salim...he's my uncle."

Khalid tilted his head in confusion, then opened his eyes wide in realization.

"The last name should have tipped me off that he was some relation of yours. I can't believe I didn't put it together."

"It's okay. We all know I'm the smart one between the two of us. Anyways, I had no idea you were interviewing for my uncle until last Sunday. He was already impressed with you; I just threw in a good word."

"So, I have you to thank for the job." He crossed his arms on the table and leaned forward, smiling.

"No, you have *you* to thank for the job. Who wouldn't want to hire a chocolate-loving financial consultant?"

He took another bite of cake to hide his grin, and I took another sip of coffee. We lapsed into a silence usually reserved for deep thinking.

I was working up the courage to tell him what I needed to say when Khalid put down his fork and looked at me. My heart started beating erratically as he held eye contact.

He looked down for a second before clearing his throat. "Listen, Noor, there was something I wanted to talk to you about." He glanced at me quickly before looking away and chuckled to himself. He rubbed the back of his neck. I perked up. He was clearly nervous, and it made me feel a lot better. I decided to test the water.

"Is this about us?" I asked tentatively.

He considered me as I considered him.

"It is," he said slowly.

"I think we're on the same page."

"Just to be clear, is that page the page where it says we both like each other and would like to see where things go?" He said it all together in one breath, like he needed to say it before someone or something stopped him.

I was so relieved. I was fully expecting nonsensical babble from me and a careful suggestion to just be friends from him. This scenario was infinitely better. I was contemplating my blessings this month when I realized that Khalid had been quiet for a while and was looking very, very worried. I hurried to rectify his misunderstanding.

"No, Khalid, I mean, yes. That's the page we're on." His relief was obvious. "But I'm only giving you two months before you have to make your intentions clear to my parents."

He grinned. "I'm okay with that. So, umm, are you going to finish your cake?" he asked.

I pushed the cake towards him. We shared the rest of it.

Twenty~Six

Saturday, May 23

Khalid: Did you reach the gate yet?

No.

I'm finishing my coffee at the cafe.

Didn't your flight start boarding
twenty minutes ago?

Yea, it's last calling now.

Do you want to get stuck with them
sending your luggage to the
luggage hold because you couldn't
find space in the overhead
compartment?

Might be too late to worry about
that now, but good point.

How was saying goodbye to your
family?

Hessa and mom cried.

Sara and dad tried not to cry.

Leaving is hard.

You're brave each time you come
back, knowing you'll have to go
through that again.

Here's to hoping this is the last time.

I better board the plane.

I'll message you when I land.

Tuesday, May 26

What do you mean your sisters
know about me?

Khalid?

Khalid!!!

Maybe you can tell your sisters
about me now?

My sisters already know about you.

They do? When did you tell them?

After our first date at City Walk.

Mona and Hana know too.

And the girls of course.

Tuesday, June 2

Your niece is the cutest.

Send me more pictures.

Khalid sent 24 images

You're the best.

Monday, June 15

Do you know where Ahmed is?

Why would I know where Ahmed is?

You're the one married to him.

You should know.

He's sulking.

What'd you do?

Nothing! All I said was that I
couldn't wear the matching shirt
because there's a huge ketchup
stain on it. Which he put there, by
the way.

Oh no.

He was really excited about you
guys matching tonight.

Then he shouldn't have gotten
ketchup on the shirt. Why are you
up so early by the way?

Nerves. Who knew dissertations
didn't write themselves?

One sentence at a time. You can do
this.

Tuesday, June 30

Baba: I've asked your amo and he
says Khalid is a good man. I'm
happy for you, baba. If this is what
you want, then I'll make
arrangements for the official
engagement once you're back.

Mama: His mother and I are going
to a spa this weekend.

Hessa: Mama won't take me to the
spa with her, so I'm going with
Khalid's sisters.

Sara: Can I take your white blouse?

Wednesday, July 1

HAPPY BIRTHDAY KAHLIIIIIIIIID!

Thank you! Wish you were here.

Soon!

Only four more months.

I'm counting down the days.

Sunday, July 26

How can you think that The Hobbit
is better than Lord of the Rings?

Because I like you, I'm going to let
that slide.

Wednesday, August 5

Please send more Arabic coffee.

I told you to ration it out.

I didn't think I'd be this stressed
with edits.

It's just editing.

Why is it stressful?

Because you're a perfectionist? I'm
sure it doesn't even need editing
anymore. You've been at it since
June.

I have twenty pages of graphs that
aren't aligned.

I need them to align.

How can I publish an article with
unaligned graphs?

You need more sleep.

I need more coffee!

Saturday, August 8

Check-in: you still like me, right?

I do.

Wednesday, August 19

You sent me coffee!!

Have I mentioned that you're the
best? Because you are!

I humbly accept your compliment.

No, you don't.

You're probably grinning like crazy
right now.

You can't prove it.

Wednesday, September 9

Did you find out what's missing in
your dissertation.

Yes.

And it's going to take a month of
setting up the experiment and
running assays to get the
information I need.

That pushes me a month back.

I may not finish in time now.

If there's anyone who can do it, it's
you. I'm happy to read through
some pages for editing. I'm happy
to read all of it if that's what you
need.

Monday, September 14

I can't believe I'm sitting in this
library, editing a paragraph I wrote
that makes no sense to me now
while you're in Switzerland.

Not fair!

Khalid sent 3 images

You're cruel.

I miss you.

I miss you too.

Saturday, September 26

I love you.

I love you too.

Friday, October 16

If I keep receiving emails from my
supervisor, Ghada, and all the
different contacts for the institute,
my inbox is going to demand I start
paying it.

Welcome to business. It's a lot of
Dear Sir/Madam's and best wishes.

And they respond as if they didn't
bother read the previous email.

That's why I sent the previous email!

I'd like to say you get used to it, but
you don't.

Thursday, November 5

I. DID. IT.

The dissertation has been
submitted and defended!

I'M DONE!!!!!

Congratulations Dr. Noor Saeed! I'm
so proud of you, love.

"Can I get one decaf espresso, please?" I asked as I leaned across Khalid in the car to the window closest to the man taking orders.

We were parked on the side of the road outside one of the many coffee shops on Jumeirah Road. It was mid-April, and a light breeze was making its way inside. I breathed it in. It was probably the last breeze we'd have before the humid summer months were upon us.

"Of course, ma'am. What about you, sir?"

"Do you have any tea?" Khalid asked. I snickered.

"Sorry, sir. We don't," the waiter informed my husband before leaving to place my order.

It didn't matter how often we came to this exact coffee shop—Khalid always asked for tea. His reasoning was that you never knew when they would decide to start offering tea. Except I would know. I follow their social media. It was just entertaining keeping him in the dark.

"We can get you one dirham chai from down the road, you know."

"I may as well wait until we get to your parents' house and have tea there," he said.

The waiter came back with my coffee, and we drove to my parents' house. I held my coffee in one hand, and Khalid took my other hand as he drove. It's been almost a year since our wedding, and I still melt over the simple gesture. Khalid caught me looking at our entwined hands and lifted them to his mouth to kiss the back of my hand before resting them between us again.

"Did you manage to get all your sisters to come?" I asked.

"After two weeks of navigating their schedules and finding a time that suited everyone, I did. Thanks for the help, by the way," he added sarcastically.

"You know I would have helped, but I'm so busy with finalizing all the minor details for the research institute. Ibrahim wanted to see the financial contracts with all the companies renting out lab space. It's been a nightmare getting them to sign it since Ramadan started. No one wants to do any actual work."

"I thought Ghada said they didn't need them just yet."

"Ghada didn't need them, but Ibrahim sent me the world's longest email explaining why he needed them by four pm today. Grand openings are a lot of work."

"Hey," he looked over quickly. "I'm proud of you."

"Thank you. I'm proud of me, too."

After two years of endless meetings, emails, and contracts, the grand opening of my research institute was only a few months away. I got excited butterflies every time I drove past the building that would be my domain for, basically, the rest of my life.

The first time I walked through the new and shiny laboratories on the first tour of the institute, I needed a moment to absorb the enormous realization that everything I was seeing was real and tangible and mine.

And it was almost time to open the doors. The number of interested students and researchers was overwhelming at first. But I had the institute built with a large enough capacity to accommodate everyone. Principal investigators were set up with labs and groups composed of at least five student interns at any given time.

"Are you excited?" Khalid asked.

There were many things he could have been

referring to, but since we were talking about the institute, I assumed he meant the opening.

"Excited doesn't even begin to describe how I feel. I just wish Lamya hadn't decided to have her wedding a week before opening day."

"I still blame Ahmed. He's so dramatic. Did I tell you that he told me he might die if he had to wait an extra week to marry her?"

I chuckled. It sounded exactly like Ahmed.

Lamya and Ahmed had run into each other on our wedding day. Lamya was on her way out when she tripped on her heel and fell. Ahmed was waiting for the valet to bring his car around when he witnessed the whole thing and went over to help her up. They knew of each other through me, obviously, but hadn't ever met until that day.

Both Lamya and Ahmed hounded me with vague questions about each other until I realized what was happening. Fast forward three months, and they were engaged. They got married in a hotel ballroom in the winter and now, they were so cute together it was hard to imagine a time when they weren't in love with each other.

Khalid and I cruised down Jumeirah Road in comfortable silence. I looked out the window at the passing lights and finished my coffee. I didn't indulge as often as I used to anymore, but some sacrifices are easy to make.

I placed the takeout cup down and rested my

hands on my belly, gently rubbing the almost imperceptible bump.

I'd gone into the hospital for a checkup in the middle of the work day after feeling nauseous and came out with a sonogram and decided not to go back to my sparse office in the research center. I called Khalid on my way home to our apartment while he was at work, excited to share the news with him, but he didn't answer. I sent him a picture of the sonogram and promptly fell asleep.

I woke up later to no news from Khalid. He never called me back or responded to my message, which was extremely weird behavior for him. I was about to call him when I heard the front door open. I walked to the main hall, where I found Khalid carrying a box, the hall behind him strewn with various baby items. He put the box down—which was a baby seat—and charged at me. He picked me up and spun me around, our laughter echoing in the hall. He framed the sonogram and put it on his bedside table.

"Hey, Khalid?"

"Yes, Noor."

"I'm excited."

"For what?"

"For everything."

He squeezed my hand, and I squeezed back.

"Me too."

Acknowledgments

I've read countless acknowledgments in other books and never thought I'd ever be writing my own. This journey has been surreal and would never have been possible without my support system.

The biggest thank you to my readers for giving this story a chance.

This book would not be in your hands if it wasn't for my editor, Samiha Hoque, who read the first chapters of my story and wanted more. You have been incredible throughout the entire process, and your dedication and love for this story have made the journey so much fun.

And thank you, Alex Asfour, for the best cover design I could have ever asked for.

Zizi, this story was written chapter by chapter purely for your entertainment. Thank you for asking for more chapters and not letting me stop until the story was written.

Thank you to my parents, family, and friends, who, from the moment I told them about this book, have been waiting to get their hands on it. Baba, when you told me I should consider writing a book one random afternoon, I was in the middle of writing this one.

And a special thank you to my sister, cousins, and friends who read this story before anyone else even knew about it when it was just a story on my laptop and encouraged me to keep going.

About the Author

Zainab Alhalwachi is a Bahraini molecular scientist who was born and raised in Dubai.

When she's not writing Arab romance stories, she's immersed in scientific research, flying to new destinations, or unwinding at home with her two demanding cats.